THE

Book of Sirius

KING

Of THE

SEA

A METAPHYSICAL NOVEL AND MUSICAL ODYSSEY

Dearest Mark,
With lots of love,
Aunty Bala
17/01/2020

notionpress
.com

INDIA · SINGAPORE · MALAYSIA

THE

Book of Sirius

KING

Of THE

SEA

A METAPHYSICAL NOVEL AND MUSICAL ODYSSEY

NANDAN GAUTAM

www.nandangautam.com

Notion Press

Old No. 38, New No. 6
McNichols Road, Chetpet
Chennai - 600 031

First Published by Notion Press 2019
Copyright © Nandan Gautam 2019
All Rights Reserved.

ISBN

Paperback: 978-9952-8348-0-2
Hardcase: 978-9952-8348-1-9

~

Dedicated to Bharat Thakur.
And all my friends aboard the ship,
Wherever they may be . . .

~

CONTENTS

THE MUSIC

~

THE KING OF THE SEA

~

01 I Will Be Free 2:32
    Nandan Gautam: Spoken Word, Voice, Synth, Strings
    and Bass Programming

02 Hold on to Your Sails 4:52
    Nandan Gautam: Vocals, Lyrics, Synth Solos, Synth, Drum
    and Bass Programming

03 The Ship of Desires (feat. Tony Das) 8:00
    Nandan Gautam: Voice, Synth, Drum and Bass Programming
    Tony Das: Electric Lead and Ambient Guitars

04 The Book of Sirius 7:14
    Nandan Gautam: Voice, Keyboard, Synth Solo, Synth, Strings,
    Drum and Bass programming

05 You Escape Yourself (feat. Tony Das) 4:20
    Nandan Gautam: Voice, Synth, Drum and Bass Programming
    Tony Das: Electric Lead and Ambient Guitars

06 Far Away 2:28

Nandan Gautam: Spoken Word, Voice, Keyboard, Synth and
Strings Programming

07 Our Moment in Time (feat. Tony Das) 5:30

Nandan Gautam: Voice, Synth, Drum and Bass Programming
Tony Das: Electric Lead and Ambient Guitars

08 The Glory of Love (feat. Ilia Maisuradze) 6:31

Nandan Gautam: Voice, Spoken Word, Synth, Drum
and Bass Programming
Ilia Maisuradze: Electric Lead Guitar

09 In the Land of Eternal Fire (feat. Ilia Maisuradze
and Sabir Memmedov) 9:09

Nandan Gautam: Voice, Synth, Drum, Percussion
and Bass Programming
Ilia Maisuradze: Electric Lead and Ambient Guitars
Sabir Memmedov: Clarinet

10. I (feat. Sabir Memmedov). 4:53

Nandan Gautam: Voice, Spoken Word, Keyboard, Synth,
Strings and Bass Programming
Sabir Memmedov: Clarinet

11. The King of the Sea (feat. Tony Das and Bharat Thakur) . . 6:57

Nandan Gautam: Voice, Synth, Percussion and Bass Programming
Tony Das: Electric Lead and Ambient Guitars
Bharat Thakur: Spoken Word

~

Personnel

Nandan Gautam: Voices, Spoken Word, Synth, Beats, Bass and
Drums Programming (All Tracks)

Tony Das: Electric Lead & Ambient Guitars (Tracks 2, 3, 5, 7, 11)

Ilia Maisuradze: Electric Lead & Ambient Guitars (Tracks 8, 9)

Sabir Memmedov: Clarinet (Tracks 9, 10)*
Bharat Thakur: Spoken Word (Track 11)

~

ALL TRACKS COMPOSED, ARRANGED AND PRODUCED BY NANDAN GAUTAM

*Clarinet Solos based on 'Vagzali', Azerbaijani Folk Song
Mastered by Alex Sterling, Precision Sound Studios, New York

~

THE DIVINE FLAW

~

01 On the Way to Heaven [Quién Sabe](feat Amit Heri) . .   6:48
*Nandan Gautam: Voice, Vocals, Lyrics, Synth, Drum, Percussion
and Bass Programming*
Amit Heri: Electric Lead and Rhythm Guitars

02 The Divine Flaw (feat. Rainer Brüninghaus
and Antonio Sanchez) 11:32
*Nandan Gautam: Voice, Synth, Strings, Percussion, Beats
and Bass Programming*
Rainer Brüninghaus: Piano
Antonio Sanchez: Drums and Drum Solo

03 The Endless Journey I-II (feat. Ananth Menon,
Chad Wackerman and Antonio Sanchez) 6:36
Nandan Gautam: Voice, Synth, Beats and Bass Programming
Ananth Menon: Electric Lead Guitar
Chad Wackerman: Drums (Part 1)
Antonio Sanchez: Drums (Part 2)

04 The Forsaken (feat. Antonio Sanchez) 7:03

  Nandan Gautam: Voice, Synth, Percussion, Beats and Bass Programming

  Tom Schuman: Keyboards and Keyboard Solo

  Antonio Sanchez: Drums

  Bharat Thakur: Voice

~

Personnel

Nandan Gautam: Voices, Spoken Word, Synth, Beats and Bass Programming (All Tracks)

Rainer Brüninghaus: Piano (Tracks 2, 5)

Tony Das: Electric Lead and Ambient Guitars (Track 5, 9)

Amit Heri: Electric Lead & Rhythm Guitars (Track 1)

Ilia Maisuradze: Ambient Guitars (Track 7)

Sabir Memmedov: Clarinet (Tracks 6, 10)

Ananth Menon: Electric Lead Guitar (Track 3)

Antonio Sanchez: Drums (Tracks 2, 3, 4, 6, 7, 10, 11)

Tom Schuman: Keyboards (Tracks 10, 11)

Bharat Thakur: Voice (Track 11)

Chad Wackerman: Drums (Tracks 3, 5)

~

ALL TRACKS COMPOSED, ARRANGED AND PRODUCED BY NANDAN GAUTAM

Mixed by Sudharsan Krishnakumar, Raghu Dixit Studios, Bangalore

Mastered by Alex Sterling, Precision Sound Studios, New York

~

Both Albums are available on all digital platforms.
You may listen to/download them for free from this exclusive weblink:
www.nandangautam.com/download

Scan the QR code below to go directly to the webpage
(iPhone users can simply point their camera at the code)

~

For Music Videos visit my YouTube Channel—Nandan Gautam

~

EXECUTIVE PRODUCER
LEYLA ALIYEVA

PRODUCER
NANDAN GAUTAM

~

AUTHOR'S NOTE

~

I started writing *The King of the Sea* in the summer of 2012. At that point, I had little or no idea of what was taking shape. But I was compelled to write, and so I did.

I had only one rule—that I would not add a single line or paragraph in between what I had already written. This book would be written sequentially. And the reader would read it in exactly the same way that I wrote it. Meanwhile, I was also creating music in my home recording studio.

My approach was unorthodox as I had no knowledge of music theory. With the help of technology, I was able to translate my musical ideas and flesh them out into physical form. It was as if I had finally found the tools with which I was free to make just the kind of music I wanted to – one that didn't fall into any specific genre but took the best elements from each. One day, as my music played in the background, it instantly resonated with the chapter that I was writing. Emotionally, as well as thematically, it was as if that song captured the essence of the feeling I was writing about.

The idea of creating a music album to accompany my book was born right there. Each song (and music video) would tell its own story… taking the reader from one place to another… and from one state of mind to another. It would take the reader into the very heart of what the characters were experiencing.

I freely took from all musical forms and genres—pop, rock, jazz, ambient, lounge, Sufi, Azerbaijani folk, and Indian music in all its breadth. I created not one but two full albums, to accompany my book. The first volume was called *The King of the Sea*, and the second—*The Divine Flaw*.

I had the privilege of working with some of the world's finest musicians. Some of them, like Rainer Brüninghaus (composer/pianist with Eberhard Weber and the Jan Garbarek Group), Tom Schuman (composer/keyboardist and co-leader of Spyro Gyra), Chad Wackerman (composer/drummer with Allan Holdsworth and Frank Zappa) and Grammy Award Winner Antonio Sanchez (composer/drummer with the Pat Metheny Group and composer of the original film score for 'Birdman') were/are an essential part of the very bands that shaped my musical sensibilities. They honor me with their presence and their endless well of musical ideas.

Others—Amit Heri, Tony Das, Ilia Maisuradze, Sabir Memmedov and Ananth Menon—were not only close friends, but incredible musicians that brought with them an intensity and emotionality combined with a melodic inventiveness that is rare to find. This music would not be what it is without each of their invaluable contributions.

The King of the Sea is all three—a novel, a journal, and a musical odyssey. It is the window to another world . . . a world where we are unafraid to dive into the depths of our soul and eventually be free from all that binds us.

That is my intention. This is my wish for you. To be free...

Nandan Gautam
April 2019

FOREWORD

~

The King of the Sea is a book that defies easy interpretation. It breaks so many rules and conventions of storytelling that the reader could easily lose his way in it. It resembles poetry or spiritual texts more closely than it does prose fiction. Its vocabulary is drenched in poetic language, and its themes are grand and eternal.

Characters speak in circles and in riddles. Narratives wander from plane to plane, making a mockery of the verities of time and space. Nothing proceeds in a linear, straight-ahead fashion. Time loops in a never-ending, bending curve. The present, past, and future are hopelessly entangled and enmeshed with each other.

Three different typefaces are used to convey the three separate dimensions in which the action of the story unfolds. One of these typefaces represents the author himself, who seems to be speaking directly to the reader and providing a kind of post-modernist, simultaneous running account of him writing this story, this book, *The King of the Sea*, and the mental and spiritual processes he goes through in his writing of it. This device is a very self-referential, very experimental, iconoclastic approach to writing—the very opposite of accepted, traditional storycraft.

There are no shortcuts to understanding—or even following the action of — the central message of *The King of the Sea*. All readers will have to do exactly as I did—read, read some more, and keep reading. Eventually, some part of this exceedingly unique narrative will attach itself to the reader that will, in turn, illuminate some other part of the story, and so on, and so on.

In many ways, this is a story of contrasts, of opposites. And where there are poles, there is always the chance and hope for unity between those opposites.

I advise readers to enter into this time-space resisting the urge to draw conclusions or try to connect the dots—until they connect themselves. Readers may find themselves swimming or drowning, in the sea of their own lives, wondering at the end if what they read really was a book. Or something else entirely.

Frank W. Kresen
Editor

PROLOGUE

~

"There are no rules here. We make them up as we go along," I said. "And be careful. Don't believe anyone. Especially not yourself!"

"What?" he yelled back. The wind made it hard to hear.

"Nothing," I said, realizing that what I had said, was for myself.

~

I woke up wondering what it meant—this dream I saw so sharp and clear.

Was this a story I was supposed to write?

Something was unfolding. Perhaps from another time . . . or another world . . .

~

"You escape yourself, my friend. You escape yourself."

The answer came swiftly.

~

Sometimes when you speak to yourself, you hear something in between that you don't quite understand—in a voice that's not quite your own.

~

I decided to write it all down.

~

The visions . . .

The Voice . . .

The scenes that were unfolding in my life . . .

~

Everything.

~

June 6, 2012

BOOK I

~

The last thing I heard when I walked out of that door was, "You'll be back."

I knew I wouldn't. Even though the patterns of my life spoke otherwise. There's always a moment when you know you won't be looking back. They don't come often. But when they do, you know it. Especially when they come far and between. This time it was eleven. Eleven years since I had reached a point of no return. Truly, I had forgotten life could ever change. When God doesn't give you that moment for so long, you forget that it could ever happen. And when it does, it hits you like a cold arctic breeze and stings your soul with a strange pleasure.

Was it me? Or was it some higher force that created these points in life? I didn't know. Either way, the feeling was unmatched. And for those few moments, you are fearless. You become God.

~

"What can you give your life for?" he asked, as he dug through the earth, pulling out the weeds.

"Anything," I said. "Almost anything."

He said nothing.

"Anything worthwhile." I continued.

1

"Hmmm . . ." he said, nodding his head.

"It's a short life; I might as well do something useful . . ." I explained.

"Might as well." He struck the iron bar into the earth, digging it deep. "Start work on the fields to my right. The little seedlings need to be planted. They are ready."

"Yes, my King." I replied, not sure if this was the correct way to address him.

"Call me King, as I am not your King." He pushed the bar down, breaking a piece of the earth. "I am a King without a Kingdom. And my subjects are those who love me because I am a King, not because I am their King."

"Yes. Yes, of course," I replied.

Something was strange about the entire conversation.

~

"How do I do this?" I thought. "I'm tired and burnt out . . ."

"Let go, my friend. Just let go," The Voice said, calmly.

"I've come too far. It's impossible." I replied. "Even letting go is too difficult."

"It's just habit. That's all . . . habit."

"I'm ready to give up." I put my head back and let out a deep breath. "I'm just not strong enough to break this habit."

"Good." The Voice was steady. "Then the habit will break you."

My mind failed to comprehend the statement.

"It's only when you're utterly hopeless that you can even begin to feel the immeasurable strength that you possess." The Voice spoke. "Not the strength to move mountains, but the realization that nothing is actually happening and that everything is perfect. This is the ultimate strength. From here will spring action without fear, without worry for the future, with a confidence not in the outcome but a confidence in life itself. Remember, you are the chosen one, and He doesn't make mistakes."

~

My heart started to beat faster.

~

These were strange days.

Sometimes I would hear things as I was waking up, in the state between wakefulness and sleep. Or get a glimpse of things that would happen at a future point in time.

Sometimes I would jump out of bed with my heart pounding, in the middle of the night, for no reason. Sometimes, in the middle of a conversation, words would pop into my brain, which I could either say out loud or keep to myself. Mostly, I did the latter. Then there were the impulses that made me do things I wasn't quite sure why I was doing. Either my mind was playing games with me or I was going crazy.

"Not a chance," The Voice said. "A greater force has tuned into you and is leading you towards a destination that your conscious mind is still unaware of . . . You're not crazy. Remember that."

~

I knew I wasn't.

~

Was it The Voice of God? I wondered.

That's what I wanted to believe.

~

"The answers will come . . . you will be guided . . ." I told myself.

"Be careful," The Voice said, before I could finish the sentence. "I don't always guide you."

I could hear it clearly.

~

I sometimes take you away from yourself.
I push you as far as you can possibly go.
It's the surest way to find yourself again.

~

It was easier to hear The Voice when I spoke to myself.

~

That evening, entire crops had been lost. The rains, instead of nourishing the land, flooded the soil and washed away everything, leaving behind dead slush.

"Let's celebrate," he said.

We looked at him with astonishment.

"Open up the casks, and bring out your instruments," he announced aloud, with a sense of achievement and authority.

They all walked away, wondering.

I stayed back, staring at his face, trying to decipher the event.

"If you cannot celebrate loss, you have already lost, my friend." He smiled. "A King celebrates victories and defeats alike. That's why he is a King."

~

"So you are a romantic at heart after all . . ." I said to her.

"I don't know. I think you know me better. Better than myself."

"Do I?"

"Yes. You do."

"Then it's settled forever. You are a romantic, even if you believe otherwise."

"If you say so," she laughed.

~

We walked to the local tavern that night, a few miles away from the farmlands. It was a weekly ritual we had grown accustomed to, even though a heavy head was certain to follow the next morning.

"By the end of the season, we will all be rich," said my comrade. "The King is right. I have never seen grapes so large and sweet in my life."

"I'm tired of hope. Very, very tired," I said. "I want to live just for the day . . . dreams and hopes can destroy your life . . ."

"We live for the future, friend. I must hope . . . for this life, what we live, is no life," he said, as we quaffed our cups through the night and drifted into a world that was ours and ours alone.

~

The prison of today is your eternal freedom.

~

"So, what are you going to do now with your life? And where will you go?"

I was speaking to myself.

5

"I don't know."

"You have to do something. Anything."

"I don't know. I really don't."

I was quiet.

~

Not knowing isn't a bad thing. It can have mysterious effects on your life.

~

I was quiet.

~

The universe can't react to you anymore.

~

"What happens then?"

~

See for yourself. Don't you enjoy being surprised?

~

I smiled to myself. There was no doubt about that.

~

The quietness of the day lay like a blanket over the city. I could feel it for miles.

Even to speak a word felt like a strain. Thoughts flitted through my mind like little insects in an expanse of a clear night sky.

This was one of those days when you wanted to feel something. You wanted to color this silence. With joy or sadness or peace. Anything . . .

But it was just silent. So silent that nothing could be done. Without air, how could there be any breeze . . .

~

The force can work through anyone, my friend. Recognize this.
Be humble. Become small. God works through one and all.
One and all.

~

I looked into the mirror, and I could see that, beneath the subcutaneous fat, were muscles. Beneath the belly was a strong abdomen.

Perhaps I had mistaken my exterior for my interior.

But it was not so. I was actually strong.

~

"To get something you've never had, you have to do something you've never done," a friend said, repeating a quote from somewhere.

"To be something you've never been, you have to embrace all that you are today, and all that you reject within yourself," I replied.

It wasn't me—I knew. It was The Voice.

~

Who are you?

~

It doesn't matter. It's what I do that matters.

~

What is that?

~

It's a specialized kind of surgery.

~

I divide you.

~

Into two.

~

Now you will haunt yourself for the rest of your life, till you become one.

~

Every time I wanted to run away from where I was, I asked myself two questions: What am I running away from? And where am I running to?

I could never get past these two questions.

No answer was good enough for me anymore.

And as the years passed, the thought of running away gradually became a flight of imagination.

~

A time will come when I will tear you into shreds. I will demolish the very ground that you stand upon.

~

No belief will survive it. Nothing will go unobserved from that day on.

~

You will be unable to rebuild yourself as you are, my friend.

~

Take it. Like a man.

~

You're being prepared for that day.

~

The Wedding at the Village

~

"How's your love life these days . . . ?" He called at half-past four in the morning and asked. He sometimes called at odd hours, asking questions that were clearly out of context. At least that's what they appeared to be. But now, after thirteen or more years as His student, this was common. And nothing was truly out of context. Especially anything to do with *Him*.

"Nothing," I said. "Nothing's happening."

"Be open, be open. You're stuck in another time." He put the phone down.

~

It happened on the day they got married, when I was seventeen. It was a small gathering, of not more than sixty or seventy people. And there was much wine flowing and merriment in the air that night. The musicians sat on one side, and the couples gathered together at the center to dance. My brother and his newlywed wife sat on the swing decorated with flowers while the children swung it back and forth.

"Not so fast," he scolded them. "We'll get a headache."

"They're just children," she said to him softly. "Let them be."

He smiled. She smiled back. "Come, let's dance," she said, holding his hand and getting up from the swing.

"Give me a few minutes. I will need a large cup of wine before I can dance to the songs of those sorry musicians," he laughed. "You go ahead, love. I'll be with you in a minute."

She smiled and ran towards me. "Let's dance. Come on. Have I ever danced with you?"

"Perhaps not." I replied, as she held my hand and dragged me to where all the couples were dancing.

"Where do these songsters come from, exactly?" I asked her.

She laughed. "They're terrible, aren't they?"

And we held hands and danced.

And I smelled her hair for the first time.

And when the dance was over, it was done.

~

You cannot touch the unknown, my friend. The unknown can touch you, however.

~

We created the perfect prison for you. You can't get out of this one, my friend. You will be free now. From all that binds you.

~

"I cannot hate you," The Crazy One said to Him.

He said nothing.

"You will not make me hate you," she said. 'I do not want to be free of you."

"But you will. I assure you. From all of this," He repeated, with an unexpected kindness in his voice. I could see it clearly, as I stood at a distance, watching. She would be free. Someday. I knew she would.

~

We had worked hard on the rocky lands that day, breaking the rocks and pulling them out of the ground. Finally the land was ready to be tilled. We ate our supper under the tree that day, tired from the day's work but happy with ourselves.

"Why is it, my friend, you speak of everything but that which tears your heart apart?" The King rarely spoke, but today he asked me questions that not a soul had asked me on these farmlands. "Why is it that you never speak of love?"

"Love was forgotten long ago," I replied. "I search for something else now. For that which is eternal. For what good is that, which like a butterfly, stays on your shoulder for a few moments, or even years, before it flies away or dies? What good is it? I want to know God."

"Ah, but my friend, it's this little butterfly that wreaks havoc on your soul. Perhaps this very creature will lead you to the eternal." The King looked up at the darkening skies. "Perhaps he whom you wish to meet is the one who sent this winged creature your way, to sit on your shoulder . . ."

~

Everything is perfect. I control everything. Even you. So relax.
Rest in this knowledge.
My work will be done, one way or another. I cannot fail.

~

"These are sacred grounds. And that is why what we grow here will be the sweetest and the most succulent." The King walked through the valley and took note of the land. "Water will be found here, so keep digging," he said, as he plunged the long iron bar in his hands into the soft soil. "And treat each plant as your child, for it needs your love as a newborn baby needs a mother's love."

We started planting that day, towards the western side of the land.

"I want all ten acres planted by sunset. I shall cook for you while you work, and what you eat will nourish your body as well as your soul, for this meat will be cooked for six hours, till it is more soft and succulent than what you may have eaten from your mother's own hands. Now get to work, my friends. There is much to be done."

~

Become suspect. Be watchful of all that is happening around you. It is coded. It has a purpose. And it will not necessarily fall into your framework of logic.

~

"What you ask of us cannot be done. It is impossible." I threw the plowbar down and walked away, towards the trees, where the path to the quarters began. "You are no ordinary King, I know, but I am an ordinary servant. And these hands cannot perform miracles."

"Why don't you eat dinner and go to bed if you are tired?" the King replied. "And remember, neither you nor my people are servants. They are my family, my subjects, and they will perform miracles if I so wish."

"I'm not hungry. I haven't truly been since I got here," I said.

"Then drink your wine. Or go back to your home, to your mother. She needs you, perhaps," he answered firmly.

But I had already left home. No one needed me there. And these farmlands had become the only home I knew.

~

Don't be angry with those who are slow to understand.
Don't be angry with those who are against themselves.
Avoid anger with the thick-skinned.
For they are all parts of you.
Start by being patient with yourself.
Embrace who you really are, for there lies the key to your soul's freedom.
The only duty you have is to yourself.
And from your freedom will emerge the key for another.

~

The dregs of your personality will emerge.
From within you, and all around you.
So don't go to war with the world.

And don't go to war with yourself, my friend, even though I know you will.
For what you reject outside of you is none but you.
And what you believe is you, is not you.

~

Embrace, embrace
All that is happening within.
And all that is happening in the world.
Here lies the answer.

~

"Your sense of duty will be your undoing, my friend," the King said, looking at the fields as the sun was setting.

"Timing is everything," he continued. "It is all going like clockwork, and nothing is out of place. Trust me." He smiled a proud smile. "We will feed the whole world tomorrow, my friend, and intoxicate those who have the appetite."

The word "trust" had become alien to my soul. I could hear it like a long-forgotten word whose meaning I could not comprehend anymore. Yet these words were my only solace in this desert, where I trudged along with bruised feet, longing for a drop of water where none was to be found. It was now a matter of survival, not trust.

~

"You went to war, didn't you? With yourself," I asked myself. "Even though you were told not to."

"I had to." I replied. "I had to."

"And did you win?" I asked.

"I don't care," I replied, a part of me knowing that this was not the answer that ever led to anything good.

"Put your weapons down. Nobody ever wins. It hasn't been done."

I knew I was telling myself the truth. There would be no victory here. But for now, I was putting nothing down.

~

The dogs howled every evening, and their howls could be heard all across the farmlands—the loud ones from the north and the distant ones from the southwest.

"I am leaving," he said to the King. "I can no longer stay here."

"Why?" asked the King. "What is it you seek?"

"I don't know, but I know I cannot stay here."

"The day you commit to this land, my friend, or anything at all, with all your heart, without hope of success, but faith in God, is the day you will find what you seek." He looked up at me. "Perhaps your time has not come. Not yet."

"I think it has," I replied softly, with my head down.

"Will you be going back home?"

"No. I will be moving onward, to the north, where they say lies a magical forest where no sun ever touches the land but where fruits grow plenty and wild. There are sages there with powers that we know not here. They say the lord has blessed that forest."

"Ah, yes—that forest," the King replied.

"It does exist then? Am I correct?"

"It does for sure, beyond these hills, towards the northwest. Good luck, and God be with you. Do come back when you are tired of traveling. Don't forget: you always have a home here."

"Thank you," I said. "Thank you for all that you have given."

And I took one last look at the farmlands that I hoped had taught me every-thing I needed to know for my journey ahead.

~

BOOK II

~

I jumped out of bed at five in the morning, and the words echoed loudly in my head like never before. "The ship of desires, the ship of desires . . ."

I could see it. As clear as day . . .

~

The Ship of Desires

~

This was no ordinary ship. It was fueled by desire, the collective desire of all who lived on that ship. And if even one of those one hundred and thirty-six shipmen felt no desire or began to lose hope, the ship was slower for it. In the summer, when the men basked in the sun and played songs till the early hours of the morning, the ship sailed forth at breakneck speed. But in the cold winters, when they huddled up next to each other for warmth, the ship slowed down considerably.

"Wake up, fellow men! Wake up!" The Captain yelled for all to hear. "This is no time to sleep. For the longer you sleep, the longer we will take to reach our *destination. Be hopeful. Drink and keep yourself warm. We have a long way to go, and we must not lose faith!"*

"But, Captain," spoke out one young lad who couldn't contain himself. "This ship never reaches anywhere. All aboard this ship have never seen land but live in the hope that they will one day. Pray tell me: Have you, O Captain?"

"I have seen more than you can imagine, young lad," The Captain said. "Look around, will you . . . the sea waits to take you in . . . we have no choice but to carry on ahead . . ." He paused for a moment, as if waiting for us to take in the words. "If every man on this ship felt this way, we would come to a halt. And I'll be doggoned if this ship slows down, leave alone stops, on my command. It never has since the day I took charge, and it never shall till I die."

"But will you, O Captain, will you . . . die one day?" the lad asked impertinently. The others, too, were waiting for the answer.

"One day, I will. One day," The Captain said proudly. "But not before I make sure one of you is captain of this ship!"

"But none here know of a time when you weren't captain," he said. "I have asked every shipman on board. And as long as they can remember, it has always been you. Perhaps you don't die, sire. And neither will we. Perhaps we are all immortal, as truly, nothing has changed on this ship in years. It may be decades; I do not know, for time itself appears to have abandoned us."

The Captain frowned but was silent. I had spoken my worst fear aloud. I feared this was how we would live for eternity. And that death was our only escape.

And the shipmen, too, were curious. They awaited The Captain's answer with equal eagerness. For they toiled hard through the moist rains, the cold winters and the turbulent seas without the slightest idea of where they were headed.

"We live on hope, comrades—hope." He spoke to all now. "If this dies, then your ship will stop sailing. And you will be stuck here for eternity without ever seeing a single grain of sand. It is all there, written in those tattered old books down below in the hull. So raise your cups and drink your wine so that you have the strength in your hearts to carry on when the sun is weak and your bodies are stiff. And listen not to this ignorant young lad who will lead you straight into the gateway of hell. He knows nothing of this world or these treacherous seas. This ship must sail. It must. We have no choice in this matter. Know this once and for all."

The lad was quiet. It was the first time he had spoken to The Captain like this. And even though he hadn't gotten an answer to his question, he was happy that he'd spoken his heart today. He went to the lower deck, pouring himself a cup of wine. He took out his lute and strummed a tune while the sun set in the distance and the ship sailed towards a destination that no man he knew had ever seen with his own eyes.

What if we set up the sails, and let the winds carry us wherever they will? he thought. They would take the ship somewhere, surely. Perhaps God would have no choice but to guide the ship. And he slept with this thought, which slowly became a wish and a dream in his heart.

The ship sailed ahead swiftly that night.

~

I will be free, my love.

I will.

I will be free to love you,

I will be free to lose you.

Free to keep you in my heart as long as I wish, without hearing so much as a word from you.

Free to dream about you, and never wake up.

Free to forget you, and know that nothing is ever lost.

Free to leave you, and find a place in your heart forever.

Free to wait for you, without really waiting.

Free to live, without ever striking an argument with my heart.

I will be one, my love.

I will be free.

From me, and from you.

And from me and you.

~

"It has always been about you," she said. "It's about your journey, your life,
Him . . . and your love for me. I wonder if you even know me."
I said nothing.
Wasn't this the case with everyone? I thought to myself.
And what did love have to do with knowing someone . . . either you felt it,
or you didn't.

~

*The next morning, at half-past four, I awoke to the loud sounds of the ship
bell. The ship creaked and swayed while the water splashed into the ship from the
sides, blurring our eyes and peeling the skin off our hands when we held our oars.*

*"Get to your places, my lads," The Captain yelled. "And pull the sails down
immediately! Else this ship will sink!"*

*The Captain knew how to strike fear in the hearts of the men in an instant. He
had said one night after one too many drinks, "Till I am alive, my friends, this ship
cannot sink. It's impossible!" He had laughed when the men discussed the previous storm that had practically brought down the ship to its side. But besides me,
they were all drunk, so the conversation was mostly unheard. When I brought up
these words to The Captain the next day at breakfast, he simply said, "Hmmm"
and nodded faintly. I knew I would get no other answer from him.*

Presently, I took my place at the lower hull of the ship. The Captain knew exactly who would make the best rowmen and who would best handle the sails. Both needed strength, that was for sure, but the sailsmen needed instinct. They had to smell the winds before they worked the sails. They had to be alert all the time. Rowmen like us mostly worked hard during our shift, but once that was over, we were free to drink, sing, and dance. The sailsmen enjoyed no such time, for a part of them was always up there, with the sails. Their hands held an invisible mast all the time, even in their sleep. And that was why their sleep was light . . . and they dreamt a slew of dreams.

But this was the season when the winds and rains lashed at us every other day while we worked hard to keep ourselves afloat. Loud voices came from everywhere, but they paled and faded against the roar of the sea as it slapped the ship from all sides.

"Alright, lads," said The Lead Shipman, with a smile on his face. "It's time to show mother nature what we are." He seemed to enjoy this battle with the sea. At nights he drank the most, but during the day, he could row like a horse and work the sails with equal dexterity. It was no wonder The Captain had chosen him as Lead Shipman of the ship.

And we sang and rowed with all our might.

"Hold on to your sails.
You will not lose me.

Hold on to your sails.
It's not what you see.

It's now or never, my friend.
Just what can you be.

Hold on to your sails,
Eternally."

While my arms ached and throbbed, it was this song that echoed through the hull. It cut through the thunder and lightning and set us free for a moment, even as death had tried us many times and failed.

~

Surrender, and you will see miracles. Find peace in the storm,
and I will show you the way.

~

I know I cannot break your heart, I know.

I know I don't occupy the whole of it to shatter it.

But one day I will take a little piece and fling it . . . far away.

Far away into the seas that not even I will be able to find it.

For this piece will carry the whole of me.

And you will shed a tear from the corner of your eye.

Just one tear, in which is contained the whole sea.

The whole sea.

The whole of me.

~

I noticed within myself the seed of vengeance. I wasn't proud of it. But sometimes you were born a certain way, and nothing could change that. Anger, like love, could hijack my entire self.

~

"So if I cannot help myself, and no one else can help me, where does that leave me?" I put forward a philosophical question.

"Just accept," an old teacher from school said, as we sat around the table, eating dinner. "That's all. Accept yourself. There's nothing else one can do." He smiled a broad smile.

21

Who just spoke? I wondered. It wasn't what he had said, but how he had said it that gave me a strange feeling.

~

Agents of the Light

~

He had a dream that night.

She wore a soft white gown, and through the morning sunlight he could see her, floating within the seams of that dress like an angel. And she came to his bed and sat down next to him, placing her hands on his cheek, her fingers soft, like the petals of a newly born rose.

"Wake up, my friend, wake up. For it is late, and there is much work to be done on this ship," The Lead Shipman said, as softly as he could, seeing that he was in a deep slumber.

When he awoke, he could not tell if it had been a dream or whether it had really happened. He looked around the cabin, through the small windows, to see nothing but the swaying waters. But his heart was beating fast, and his head was heavy with a wine he had never drunk in this life. Was it possible to dream of things a man had never seen or touched?

~

You will not believe in me. You will become the miracle.

And then you will know me.

Then you will know who I am.

~

There are two kinds of willpower: the will to push ahead despite all obstacles, and the will to hold on to something despite all the pain.

You will know who you are. And this will be used for the work.

~

What work? I wondered. But there was no time to think. I kept writing.

~

A long time ago, I placed your feet on two different boats, one beside the other. I set both of them asail, knowing that it was a matter of time before they parted ways, by which time you would be unable to get either foot off its boat.

The day will come when they will have to part.

~

It wasn't a pleasant metaphor. But that's what I saw.

~

Try to keep your head down when you are in front of Me.

Your ignorance is acceptable, but in your arrogance, you will have closed the doors of your heart and lost the way to heaven.

The ignorant must naturally behave like this, you may think.

All I can say is: When encountering that which you cannot comprehend so easily, avoid jumping to conclusions.

Many an intelligent soul I have seen, too quick to believe
in their own intelligence.
Be patient, for it is the quality of the wise.

~

This, I understood.

~

Love is the passage that will deliver you to freedom, my friend.
Even as it bleeds your body till you can hardly move your limbs
and tires your mind till it freezes.
It is love and only love that shall set your soul free.
It's the only bridge to heaven in your world, which has become a marketplace.

~

Yes,
This butterfly will lead you to your deepest fears.
And to your greatest moments of joy.
Places you have never been and lands that you know exist
but have no faith you will ever see.

~

You know nothing of the joys of love, my friend. Nothing.
What you believe you tasted, what you believed you ate,
was merely the fragrance that I sent your way.
The feast yet awaits you, my friend.

24

~

And we shall one day eat together and share the sweet wine
and warm bread of life.

One day we shall.

~

When love floods your heart, my friend,
Even a street whore becomes your wife.

~

I kept writing. Without a break.

~

I will throw you to the high seas. I will fling you like a leaf on waves so large,
you will certainly meet death. It will not be easy, my child. During this time,
remember Me. And Me only. For only My name will make your body light as
you move through the darkness.

~

"Sing my name," The Voice said. "Sing it in your heart. And let this song play
in your heart forever."

~

You will have to come naked to this temple. You will come with fear, with
trepidation, and faith in your heart. One day you will come.

~

This temple lies at the bottom of the sea, where none breathe.
This is where the sacred meeting takes place.

~

I bled you dry not to kill you but to fill your veins with wine instead.

I destroyed the synapses of your mind not to make you stupid
but to make you receive His instructions clearly.

I broke your legs because I wanted you to fly.

~

The lines were coming faster than I could write.

~

There will come a time where I will ensure you feel nothing towards me.
It may start with loathing.

~

Whatever we may have done for each other is insignificant,
as it will all come to pass.

This is necessary so that your eyes turn within, as I will not get in the way
between you and yourself.

It is my foremost duty and task given to me by my Creator.

~

"He wasn't talking to you," The Strange One whispered in my ear, immediately after He had screamed at me. "The anger had to be released."

Maybe she was right. Maybe.

~

What one cannot do, He has to do for them.

And what cannot be heard by you will be told to another in your presence so you may listen in.

~

Sometimes, words enter you without your own knowledge.

~

Don't be angry with me. I am not the cruel one.

It is you who is cruel to yourself. It is you who denies you yourself.

I am the amplification of this.

I rub it in your face so that you can face it.

~

Grammar is for correctness.

Language is for communication.

But My words are forged to strike your heart.

~

There will be no exchange of currency here.

What I feel is immeasurable.

What you are is immeasurable.

You don't earn grace with good behavior.

Nor do you lose it with bad behavior.

There is no such thing, no such thing.

Simply be true to your self.

~

"Stop waiting for the promised land, my lads. For there, too, have you toiled and sweated for many lives. There, too, have you drunk wine every day, and there, too, have you waited for a blue sea like this where you think not of tomorrow and live for today." He laughed.

The shipmen laughed with him and made merry that night. "Live for today, I say, and dance the night until your legs cannot hold you!" The Lead Shipman shouted as they played their instruments and beat the tables with their cups full of wine.

I sat next to The Captain and asked, "But what of love? We know nothing of love here."

"Love is a butterfly, my lad. It sits on your shoulder for few seconds and flies away." He quaffed a cup of wine. "Seek the eternal in this moment. No other can help you in finding happiness. No other."

The Captain was right. Everything was passing. Like the moments of joy he felt when a new melody found its way into the lute. After a few repetitions, the song, however beautiful, wasn't new anymore. But he still returned to the lute again and again, in search of one that he would perhaps never tire of.

"If you truly knew of love, young lad, all dreams of lovers will disappear." He sipped his wine and looked at me from the corner of his twinkling eyes.

~

"Do you love me?" I asked. We sat on the small porch of their house, facing the village square.

"Yes, I do love you," she replied.

"But you love him, too."

"More than anything in the world."

I was quiet. I didn't like what I was hearing.

"I can only speak my truth," she said. "You will have to find yours."

I had to. I had to. For this was no way to live.

~

No matter how much he tried or wanted to, he could never play the same song again. And he certainly couldn't play along with the songs that his fellow shipmen sang every single day. All he did was sit with the instrument and pluck its strings until a melody began to form. They were strange, angular melodies that only a few sailors would enjoy listening to, after having one too many cups of wine. "Where's the rhythm?" The others would ask. "You can't dance to this!"

He would quietly walk to the upper deck, where few men walked or gathered. There he would sit quietly, at sunset, and strum his lute into the night. The notes of his lute would mix with the loud but distant sounds of laughter, the cups clanging and the sound of boots hitting the deck of the ship. And oddly enough, all these different sounds and voices became part of one grand song, and the notes that came out of the lute those nights spoke in a language that was not part of this world at all.

~

The mind of The Winemaker was a mystery to us all. But he kept us in good spirits with the finest of wines. His ability to break open the perfect cask of wine to suit the mood of the shipmen, along with his good cheer, was certain to lift your spirits no matter how bad the food was or how stormy the weather got. When I first had a wine too many and after much vomiting tried to keep down the burning acid that rose up from my stomach, it was The Winemaker who brought me an odd-tasting concoction. "This should stop the burning immediately," he said, with a broad smile on his face. "Take some; take some."

Not once did he ever get drunk, no matter how many cups of wine he quaffed with us. And not once did he lose the smile on his face, no matter what happened on this ship. "Carry on, my friend, carry on playing," he told me every evening, as I would uncover the lute and strum a meandering tune. "Care not if an audience listens to you. Listen to yourself as you play; that is enough." And he moved his head from side to side no matter what I played, how I played or, for that matter, even if I paused for a moment. His head continued to move to an invisible rhythm that was entirely his own.

~

Often, past midnight, when we all sat around the table, playing cards and drinking wine, The Captain would look at me and say something that didn't quite make sense.

"I don't understand," I replied.

"Learn to be quiet when I speak not to you," he said. "Looking at you is not an indication that what I say is for your ears. It reaches those whom I wish it to reach."

Who was he talking to? I wondered, looking around.

~

"Everything is training," The Strange One said. "Nothing but training, so that you can be strong in the face of accusations."

"I've let Him down," I said.

"You haven't."

I wanted to believe that. But I couldn't . . . whether it was true or not.

~

I always kill a dozen birds with one stone. Not one or two.

~

It is I who gifted you this love. Live with it, but let go all else that you seek from it. For what you seek is your undoing. Not what you feel.

~

That night, tears streamed down my face onto my pillow as I looked at my blistered hands and slight arms. I realized that I wasn't cut out to be a rowman at all. Neither was I nearly as good as The Lead Shipman at the sails. Truly, I was a lute player whose songs nobody wanted to hear. My shoulders were sore, my muscles ached, and the skin on my palms was perpetually bruised, despite all the oil that I poured on them each day.

I could never be like The Lead Shipman, I thought to myself. I remembered what The Captain had said to me the previous night. "Get yourself some muscles, young lad. You call yourself a man? That plucking of the lute you do all night isn't going to move this hundred-ton ship! We need men who can push. Men who can sweat all day and drink all night." I could feel the anger welling up inside me. "Why don't you wear a skirt and at least dance for my boys tonight?" He laughed, and the others laughed with him.

I was used to the others mocking me from time to time. But when The Captain did it, I seethed with rage.

"Cheer up, friend," The Lead Shipman said to me. "You know he's fond of you. You're the only one who really talks to him, who asks him questions, who listens to him into the wee hours of the night while the rest of us are drunk. Don't take all this seriously! And as for The Captain—trust him, for he and he alone can lead us to land. He alone . . ." His voice faded as he climbed the mast and sat on the crossbar, enjoying the cool sea breeze and smiling into the empty skies.

~

As we awoke that morning, the smell of spring caught us by surprise. It was two weeks too soon. The sun sparkled through the clouds, and the seawater was brighter by a shade or two. Beneath the surface, we could see the red and blue fish darting around, and the sails of the ship gently swelled with the steady wind.

"We will ride this ship during the day, my friends, and drink wine at sunset. We will face the storms, my friends, and lose a friend or two to the seas. We will face disease, my friends, but laugh as our feet rot away. We will swim at night with the sharks and the dolphins, my friends, and cook them for breakfast in the morning. This is the ship, my friends, where nothing is right, but all is well. So get to your oars, and oil your hands, my lads—it's time to row. In the evening, we will break open a cask of our oldest wines," he said, leaning into the wind.

The Captain was in a good mood today. And when he was in a good mood, so were all of us. And the ship sailed swiftly ahead over the gleaming waters.

~

BOOK III

~

The Voice in the Sea

~

Every ship has its leper, and so we had ours. "Sire, ask us what you want of us, and we shall abide!" he cried, as he and the men sat around drinking their wine that evening. Summer was slowly giving way to winter, and the shipmen brought out their blankets and caps each day as the sun went down. The Captain pored over the charts day after day. He was the only one on the ship who could read them. "It's all in here, son; it's all in the numbers and the winds . . . we are right on course. Your services will be called upon when needed, Leper . . . when needed."

~

"Who will be the fool of the day?

Who will pray, and who will weep?

Who will laugh as he sinks to the bottom?

Who will fly over these treacherous seas?

33

Who will remember me after all these years?

Who will know The Captain as I did fear?

Who will break their shoulder today?

Who will sip this wine and stay?"

~

It was the voice of The Madman.

"Listen not to the words of The Madman," The Captain spoke out loud. "For he has been on this ship too long, too long to speak words that make sense to you lads. But speak before him, and your wisdom may spring forth as he listens."

~

And the ship moved ahead despite the onslaught of the first winter storm, which was cold and brought a hail of ice that tore through the sails.

Only The Madman laughed at the ripping sounds of the tarmac that stretched tightly across the mast of the mainsail. The Captain stood still, knowing that much work had to be done the following day. And it was this very Madman who could climb to the very top of the mainsail and sew it together.

None else on this ship could climb the vertical pole that touched the sky at the highest point of the ship. Perhaps The Captain could, but we had never seen him do it.

The Madman quietly climbed to the very top of the mast, as only he could, and spoke loud and clear from there.

"I have been here too long, my friends, too long. And not even The Captain hears me nowadays. You all have youth on your side, and all I have is my madness. If The Captain will not hear me, then I shall not speak ever again. It is my promise. And if my listening to you all brings forth your own riches, so be it. So be it. I shall henceforth listen, and listen only."

We mumbled to ourselves. Some said The Madman wasn't mad after all. But there was no doubt in my mind that he was not like the rest of us. He was different.

~

Spill the wine you cannot drink, my friend. And drink the wine you cannot spill. For nothing is in your hands. Nothing.

~

"For god's sake, feel something, my lads." The Captain had had plenty to drink that night. "Does this ship not tire you? Do you remain happy with your drunken brawls and dirty jokes? Are you mules that live by the whip and walk with blinders, never looking up or down or left or right?"

The deck was silent, and not a soul moved for what seemed like an eternity.

"You . . ." He looked straight into my eyes. "Remind me tomorrow to be angry with you. I have had one too many cups of wine tonight, and there is too much love in my heart right now that will not allow me to raise my voice."

My heart raced a little. I took a deep breath and looked into his eyes. He turned away to fill another glass.

Sometimes two months passed by in two minutes, and sometimes two minutes took two months to pass.

Such was this ship that we journeyed on.

~

The ship rolled and swayed that night like nothing I had seen before. "Your faith will be tested tonight, my friends," The Lead Shipman said. "Keep going. Some of us won't survive this—I can assure you. But lose not hope. For those who do will surely see land in this life."

And the seas roared that day like a beast that was attacking the ship, doing all it could to bring it down.

~

What happens to the ones closest to us happens to us.
What happens to us happens to the ones closest to us.

~

The rarest of flowers will bloom on your grave, my friend.
Miracles will happen around you, even as you walk towards your end,
Love will grow in your heart even as passion dies,
And God will be reborn within the ashes of your burning body.

~

"When I am awake in the mornings, I do His work. And at nights when I am drunk, I am Him," He had said, one night after many glasses of scotch. The Crazy One knew she would never forget that line. No matter how many years had passed since He had spoken to her.

~

I leapt towards the center of the ship and heard The Captain say out loud, "Rowers, push with all your might, for today nature hath a fury that will leave this ship different than she found it. Sailsmen, hold on to your sails. As for the rest of you, pick up your buckets, keep throwing the water out. I will stand at the front of the deck and guide this ship to safety."

~

I'm ready to burn down entire crops, to teach what is needed to be learned.

Life and death are both my friends.

Gain and loss I treasure with equal measure.

~

I had a dream of her last night.

She carried a silver dagger, slender and sharp. And I lay down in her lap as she held me close, her hands on my forehead. And slowly, with a soft smile on her face, she pierced my heart and let the dagger in. As it went through, I could feel a thousand suns and moons burning and cooling my chest. My eyes closed, and my body rested like it hadn't slept for lifetimes. Like lying on the seashore while the water slowly washed away the sand from beneath.

~

Don't try to write. Instead, live. And take down notes as you do.

~

"I love you," I said to her for the first time, my head in her lap and her fingers running through my hair. "But this is it. When this ends, I will be free." I listened to what I had just said, as the tears welled up in my eyes. But neither I nor she truly knew what those words meant.

I walked away from her house that day, knowing this would not be easy.

"What happened?" my mother said, looking at me the moment I walked in the door.

"Nothing," I said, knowing that she knew exactly what I felt that day.

"Have some chicken broth. You'll feel better," she said.

"I'm not hungry," I said, even though my stomach was empty.

~

The clearest sign of The Voice was that I myself struggled to understand what the words meant.

~

When The Voice speaks, it takes no heed of time. It comes from places beyond time and reaches places beyond time. It reaches the ears of those who lived before and those who will live hereafter.

~

Do you think for a moment that I cannot speak to one and all, wherever and whenever they may exist, at this very instant?

~

This time I could feel the gentle laughter hidden in The Voice that never laughed.

~

You will rise like a balloon into the skies,

And as you go high and the air becomes thin, you will burst and be consumed by the skies forever.

~

Some surgeries are done quietly, my friend, very quietly.

For you know not what happens in the middle of the night,

While I use my needle, ever so slender, to stitch. And my knife, ever so sharp,

that it will not awaken you from your sleep.

~

A lifetime can be lived in a dream, my friend, for dreams are where days and years can pass in a moment, and a moment can feel like eternity.

~

You have nothing to give,

and there is nothing I want from you.

It is I who decides to give.

And it is I who succeeds.

It is I who will complete what I started.

It is I.

~

The Captain was right. The ship would be different after this battle. Many times, the nose of the ship would go so high into the air and crash upon the water, it felt like the bottom would give way and the ship would break in two. The thunder that followed the lightning pierced our ears as it crackled so loud we thought our ears may burst. And the lightning was so bright, so blinding . . . that when it lit up the ship for a brief moment, we all looked like ghosts, pale and white. And those images were forever inked in our hearts.

~

As I held on tight to the rope on one side and the iron bar towards my left, my sore hands could no longer hold the rope. I had thrown out as much water as I could with my bucket, but now I was just holding on for dear life. Through the years, my arms had become steadily weaker. My skin had become pale, and wine now burned my stomach. I would often wake up in the middle of the night and vomit all that I had eaten the previous day.

"Can I work on the deck?" I had asked The Captain a week ago. I can clean it and take care of the sails as well. My muscles can no longer do the job they used to."

"Do what you will," The Captain had replied. So I worked the first half of the day at the bottom, rowing with whatever strength I could gather, and the second half cleaning the deck, scraping the rust from the iron lugs and washing the sails. "Any work done with pride makes you a shipman, my friend," The Lead Shipman had said. He was perhaps my only friend, who despite never having listened to my lute, always goaded me on when I was losing hope.

~

But now I had reached the bottom of this cup. There was no drop to sip and none to throw away into the sea as my heart smiled at the thought of letting go with both my hands and becoming one of the men who were lost to the sea every year. And with that thought, my hands loosened their grip for just half a second. That was enough.

~

"The time has come to say goodbye, my dear.

Never be uncertain of me. As my love for you is eternal.

Yours forever."

I wrote a letter that day with only these three sentences.

What else was there to say?

~

"Your time has not come, lad," The Captain shouted to me as he jumped into the water and swam towards me. My arms were weak, and I knew it was a matter of minutes before the sea would swallow me. Yet, as he put his arms around my neck with a firm grip, I was both sad and relieved.

~

Now you will have to bear the burden of this love.

Now you will have to bear it.

And in bearing it shall you feel its greatness.

And in bearing it shall you become light.

~

Silence is coming.

~

Silence is coming, my friends,

Like the great sea of seas that cares not for ships or stones,

It will leave nothing the same.

All that we had and all that we didn't, it will swallow.

And we will be witness to this tidal wave

Which will leave nothing the same.

Nothing.

~

Only true brothers and sisters can be used to undo themselves. Only the true.
Only the true.

~

"Enough," The Captain said, as the storm passed and the ship settled into a steady sway. I gasped for air, and water gushed out of my lungs as he pushed my chest with his strong palms. I lay on the deck, coughing the salt water that burned all the way from my lungs to my throat. My eyes blurred, and I could faintly see The Lead Shipman. "He'll be fine, he'll be fine," he said to the others around me. I was, and I wasn't. Despite the single passing moment of safety that I felt in the grip of The Captain's arms, I wished once again that he had not saved me. And this time the wish rang through every bone in my body and from within every drop of blood left in it.

"Enough of this nonsense," he continued. "Now get back to your places, and let's move forth. Too much time has been wasted already." He tightened his belt and removed his boots, pouring out the water from inside them. "Don't ever let go of the ship, lad—you hear me? Never."

~

I saw, above to my right, The Leper, looking on from the mast where he had managed to climb. His face fell as he heard The Captain's words. For those words destroyed the one hope he lived on—to let go of the ship someday. As a man who was of little use on the ship, that was his only way out, he had figured. Today, that choice was snatched away from him as well. For he knew those words were as much for him as they were for me. And if nothing else, he knew one thing for sure—The Captain's words were not to be taken lightly. Ever.

I got up and dragged myself to the bunk where I slept. As my eyes closed, I remembered The Captain's words . . . the ship was different.

At least for me.

~

"We are all grieving for ourselves," The Strange One said. "For the selves we were but are no longer. You don't know it, but that's why you are sad for no reason."

~

Right now, you probably won't believe what is really happening to you. But in time you will. In time you will have to.

For what is done is done, and what has passed has passed.

And something else will take your place inside of you.

And you will be the proof of that.

You will be the miracle.

~

I spent six weeks in my bunk that time, during that winter, when I could have been of good use on the ship. My lungs were filled with phlegm, and every joint in my body hurt. My fingers, shoulders, elbows, knees, and back were all stiff and sore. The Ship's Healer would visit me every day, applying some black paste on my chest. "Good, good. It will bring out the dirt from inside," he would say, as I coughed, and he repeated the same procedure every day without fail. The Captain visited me not once during this time. The Leper would come by every now and then to talk to me. And his meaningless banter, even though a little crude for my taste, always cheered me up. Perhaps we sometimes needed the company of those who were least like us, to lift our spirits when they were flailing.

~

Sometimes I wondered if I had made a decision that I was not supposed to make. Was it wrong? Was there such a thing as "wrong"?

~

Don't mistake your habit for free will, my friend. For in doing so, will you have made your greatest error.

~

The day ended with a heaviness I had never felt before. Lifetimes of sadness came to me like waves, and I was sinking deep into a dark ocean that had never been touched by sunlight.

I picked up my pen and started writing.

~

Dear father,

I don't remember you. I lost you before I was two.

You were a man since you were sixteen, when you decided to be a pilot. I'm still a boy at forty-two.

You were the very best in what you did. I'm not sure what I'm doing.

You loved your family more than most could. I never created one of my own.

You were respected and loved by all around you as a warm and kind soul. I'm not sure what people think of me.

You were calm till your very last moment. I panic while I'm alive.

You were an aware soul, always grateful for what you had. I am ignorant, always wanting what I don't have.

You had compassion in your eyes. My eyes are still searching.

You let go of everything at thirty-nine to do the right thing. I haven't let go of many silly things.

There was peace in your heart the day you died, so that the innocent may live on. There is no peace here.

Yes.

You left me in a world that was in ruins.

You made me believe that *anything* can disappear in a second.

You made me build a wall around myself so that I would be happy to be alone all my life.

You made me believe that love can exist but can be taken away at any point.

Your peaceful end was my fractured beginning.

You did everything with perfection, till the end. I did everything imperfectly, right from the start.

Yet, I am your son.

And I know you loved me.

I cannot doubt your love, because that was perfect, too.

But *this* was my beginning.

I will see you on the other side . . . imperfect, boyish, uncertain.

And you will remain wise, peaceful, and loving, forever.

I accept that.

I am your opposite. And I must make my peace with this.

always your son,

always imperfect,

always searching,

just the way you perhaps knew I would be.

You had no choice in what you did.

And I have no choice but to be this way.

You gave up your life for the lives of unknown fellow men, even though you were in perfect harmony with yours.

I struggle to hold on to life . . . Perhaps I haven't come to terms with it yet.

But someday . . . I will make my peace. Someday, I will be grateful for all that I have received.

I know you wish that for me.

Until then,

Until we meet,

or not,

Always,

your son.

~

"The truth hides," The Captain said. "Even the most intelligent of you will not be able to see it." He gulped down another cup of wine. "When I'm drunk, I tell the truth. But as always, in the morning, this conversation will be forgotten."

I decided I would remember it. This time I would, I told myself. This time I would.

"Who knows when this ship will reach land, my friend?" The Captain smiled from the corner of his lips. "Who knows . . . fate is a mysterious thing, it is . . ."

"So what we are truly looking for is right here, on this ship?" I asked.

"Not quite, my friend, not quite," he replied. "Eliminate the impossible . . . and whatever remains . . ." The Captain began to slur. "I can see a man with a top hat speaking to his dear friend . . ." I could no longer understand what he spoke. Too many cups of wine, I thought. "Enough," he said. "Enough for tonight." And he stumbled towards his cabin.

~

I will send you so far away from me,
That you will come home to yourself,
And find me there.

~

I was asleep in my bunk when I realized I had slid to one side of my bed. My hands hung down from the side, and the only thing preventing me from falling were the old wooden boards that ran from top to bottom. I could feel the ship, almost lying down on its side, like a baby sleeping in her mother's arms.

I had recovered from my sickness, and though I wished to work on the ship, my bones were weak and my breath still shallow. I must have lost a stone or two, and I could see my ribs sticking out of my chest. I remembered The Captain's words from many months or years ago, "This ship will sail without me, if that is what I wish."

Today, this is what it felt like. Like there was no Captain guiding this ship. The night was still, the silence broken only by the heaving sound of water striking the hull at an angle that carried the smell of death.

And finally when the ship gently straightened, I looked out to the sea. There was no moon and no stars. She sailed under the heavy mist, without a care about her direction, as if hoping to fall off the edge of the sea, if she could. There was not a single sound that night, as the souls within slept, after eons, a dreamless sleep.

~

BOOK IV

~

You Escape Yourself

~

He walked down the moldy staircase that night, leading to the bottom of the hull. Beside the old casks that held the wine, he noticed a few large trunks with padlocks. They hadn't been touched for a long time, he could tell. They were wet and rusty, and he saw that one of them had a loose hinge. He slid his hand through the side, and his fingers tried to find something to hold on to.

He had asked his fellow sailors many months ago if any of them had ever read the texts The Captain had once spoken of. "It's a strange language, my friend, very strange," The Lead Shipman had said. "And we cannot quite make sense of it."

"Of what use are books on a ship?" The Leper chuckled.

~

Don't break the door, and don't escape.

Remain in this prison until the walls fall by themselves.

49

~

His fingers had found something. It was a text written perfectly on thin, even paper. It was undulating, with no change in color or any trace of fiber, with pages held together perfectly. He marveled at the corners that were perfectly sharp, and he wondered how the pages were cut so evenly. Just as he opened the first page, he heard The Captain's voice in the distance.

"It's time to take stock of our ship, my friends. Much damage has been done, but we must fix the masts, sew the sails, and sail again."

~

During those weeks, all I did was try to finish my duties at the earliest and return to my cabin to read. I read the sentences again and again. For although some of them were simple to understand, others swirled in my head like the birds that sometimes circled around our ship.

~

Sometimes I would drift in and out of sleep with the book on my chest, picking it up and reading a line that would take me to places I felt I had been and to places that were impossible to fathom. It was a strange book, I thought to myself, for the words would swirl in my mind for days and weeks. And gradually, but without a doubt, I could feel it changing the way I saw this ship, The Captain, and my fellow shipmen with whom I shared my life for eternity.

~

There were stretches of days so beautiful, they may have lasted weeks or months—I couldn't tell. But this was a different kind of happiness . . . one that never left a mark, because it disappeared every moment only to reappear afresh in the next . . . When there were no reasons to be happy, there was no fear of it being snatched away, either.

My friends on the ship, too, had a constant cheer about them, despite the occasional storms, our daily duties, and no sign of land whatsoever. We swam and frolicked in the clear blue waters with no care for the future. Happiness was such. And there was nothing missing in our lives. Life was perfect. Just perfect.

~

"We are all students of the land, for the land has much to teach us," The King had said.

"It teaches us that all is alive and none is dead.

And that all is dead, and nothing is alive.

That from what we call the dead can spring the living.

And that which we call living, in time, becomes the dead."

~

"It's not love," He said to me, casually. But I was not one to take any of His words casually, no matter how they were uttered. "It's some kind of obsession . . ." He continued.

It couldn't be, I thought to myself. It may be imperfect, like me. But it was still love.

~

And one day he opened a page of the book that took him to an all-too-familiar place. A place he could never really forget.

~

It was a full-moon night, sometime in December. And the winds that blew over the sea and into the port between the ships stung his face like an arctic breeze. He saw it there. The ship. It was old but strong. Like a partly wrinkled man who still had many good years ahead of him. On top of the upper deck sat The Captain, proudly, with a cup in one hand.

"Get aboard, young lads, if you want to take a journey you will be certain to forget. You will see lands you have only dreamt of and swim with fish so beautiful you will forget about the women here on land." He smiled wickedly and stroked his beard with pride. "And the wine that lies in the casks at the bottom of this ship have been made from the finest of grapes, I can assure you. They are the oldest and finest wines you will ever taste."

I was the first to get aboard that night. The drunkards all came aboard, too, for the promise of good wine was enough for them. "I had plenty of women in my time. From the youngest to the oldest. From the most beautiful to the ugliest," one strong-looking lad laughed and said, as he hopped aboard and stood at the bridge shouting out to the others who stood around curiously listening to The Captain. "Get onboard, my friends, get onboard! Enough with your miserable lives!"

"What will you pay us?" a Leper, hardly fit to be a shipman, asked The Captain.

"What you deserve, my lad, exactly what you deserve." He replied with a wink, while he did a head count of all those aboard the ship. "But do have a cup of wine before you make your final decision, my friends."

And the wine flowed, and the men assembled quickly. "One hundred and thirty-six, sire," The Leper chimed in, before The Captain could ask.

~

And he rushed to meet The Captain with the book. His body was strong and his head light, as if he had had a wine too many. He found The Captain working, fixing a broken part of the mainsail.

"Look, Captain, look! It's all here—how we got aboard and how this all started." And he began to show the book to the others around.

The Captain walked towards me. "What is this?" He frowned as he nodded towards the book I clutched in my hands.

"I found it in the trunk, near the casks down below. It speaks of love, life, and messages from far beyond." He could hardly contain his voice. "And it speaks of this ship! And how we got aboard it."

The Captain grabbed it with his strong hands and, with one sweep, flung it into the ocean. "Imagination will lead you nowhere, young lad. Nowhere," he said, staring straight into my eyes unflinchingly. "Now where were we? Get me the nails and a piece of wood twelve feet tall and six inches wide."

I ran to the side of the deck and saw the book floating on the water, shining as it caught the sun's light for a few seconds. I looked back towards The Captain, remembering his words, "Never get off this ship. Never." I wanted to say something to him. But The Captain was busy and didn't give me so much as a glance.

~

In a moment, he found himself removing his shirt and his shoes, and diving off the side into the sea. As his head entered the sea, he could feel the sound of the water, like thunder over his ears. He cut through it like a fish and swam like never before. The waters were cool and sweet. And the sun was sharp and warm on his back. He knew that, this time, The Captain wasn't coming for him.

But that didn't matter.

He was not immortal.

And land did exist.

And love, too, existed. Somewhere. Someplace.

The book was now within sight. He tried to grab it, but the waters pulled it away. He took a deep breath and swam swiftly towards the book, pushing the waters with all his strength. But each time he looked, the book was no closer to him.

Then suddenly, as if weighed down by all the water that had, by now, entered every page, the book sank. I can't lose it! I can't! he thought to himself as he took a deep breath and dived in. And as he went down, his arms and legs moving steadily, the pressure in his lungs grew. Then he heard The Voice: "It was you who wrote this book. In a future where you will experience all that you wish to."

~

The great ones can turn their students into black holes,
into which the whole universe flows.

In any direction. Forwards or backwards.

~

"How could a book come from the future?" he asked. "It's impossible."

~

For those who believe in time.

~

"But why did The Captain throw it away?" he asked. The book was sinking fast, and as he swam deeper, the pressure inside his lungs and ears was building.

~

Because it was you who wrote it.

~

I understood nothing.

~

Just remember why you came aboard this ship. Remember.

~

And as he came up, he could hear the dolphins sing. Speckles of sand glimmered and danced in front of his eyes, and he could see the light of the sun bouncing off the lucent waters.

~

"Nothing needs to change. And everything can change. That, too, is perfect." I said to her.

It was the first time that I wanted nothing from her.

Could this be true? Would this actually last?

~

He took a breath, a deep breath like he had never taken before, and saw, in the distance, the ship quietly sailing away as he started to swim swiftly towards it.

~

You will remember all that you were, all that you are, and all that you will be.
For your entire existence is but a remembrance. Not only have you loved many
a time, you have lost love in equal measure. You have been, you are . . .
a son, a father, a courtesan, and her lover.

~

This book was for you, my friend. Just for you.
That's why it was thrown into the sea.
And so is this ship. Just for you.

~

And just like that, the ship disappeared from his sight. And all that was left
was the gentle mist and the blue skies above.

~

Now you will not believe yourself, even if you try.

~

Love must grow in your heart, my friend, it must. For you know not of love
that bursts from your heart and touches one and all, the near ones and the ones
far away—the ones who sleep not a wink at night while you are sick
and the ones who pray for your demise.

You know not of that love. The love that invisibly reaches to the far corners of
this universe and touches those who lived and those yet to be born. The love that
gives life to what is dead around you and death to what feigns life.
But you will, my friend. You will.

~

He swam steadily towards the sun, in the direction of the ship, and when he looked again, it was right there, as he expected it to be. And he climbed aboard the ship, holding the rope tight and smiling all the way to greet his friends, the ones with whom he had spent many years of his life rowing, dancing, swimming, and laughing.

"Bring out the casks! Let's drink to The Captain!" he said, drying himself in the sun and squeezing the salt water from his pants. "For it is he and he alone who can take us to land!" He knew what The Captain had done. It was the only way for him to know his strength, to risk his life for what he wanted, and take a chance with death.

"To The Captain!" they all yelled after him. Any excuse to cheer or quaff a cup of wine was always welcome.

"What was in that book that made you risk your life to get it?" The Lead Shipman asked him that night. "Truth be told, I never saw you swim like that ever since we set foot on this ship."

I said nothing. What could I say? To know that we all came aboard this ship, on that cold winter night, made me feel a warmth in my heart that I had till now never felt on this ship.

For if we had a past, then we had a future as well.

And there was hope. There was much more than hope.

~

There was magic.

~

And the ship moved faster than it ever did that night.

~

It is not He or I who played this game. It is your mind that has tricked you.
I am both, its foremost agent and its worst nightmare.

For in knowing me shall you undo yourself and find out who you really are.

~

His father was a carpenter, loved and admired by all in the village for his perfectly crafted work and good cheer. "No man went away from your father without a smile on his face," his mother said to him. "Not a single man." She looked away into the distance. "That's why I loved him so."

He stood silent.

"Where are you off to now?" she asked.

"They speak of a King towards the east of the country. They say he is no ordinary King, as he tills the land with his bare hands and finds water where none exists. There are vast orchards there full of the sweetest and biggest grapes. I wish to work there."

"Yes," she replied. "And every night there are celebrations that the whole village can hear and feasts that he himself cooks for all to eat."

"You know of this King?" I asked, surprised.

"Who will get your sisters married?" she asked.

"They don't need my help, mother. You know they don't," I replied.

"But what is it you lack here?" she asked.

"Nothing, mother, nothing. All I know is that I must go. I must."

"It's her, I know," she mumbled. But I didn't hear that.

~

The last thing I heard when I walked out of that door was, "You'll be back."

~

BOOK V

~

The Invisible Ship

~

Love's grandest purpose is not its fulfillment as man and woman.
But in finding it within your heart.
So that it may grow forth.

~

Every day leads me further from my destination, because I know I travel in vain.

Every day. Every day.

I go further. Every day.

~

"Don't ever raise your voice in front of me," He said, His voice shaking with anger. "I will raze you to the ground. Do you understand?"

But I was razed already. Some words don't just hit you. Especially when they come from Him. They destroy a part of you forever.

Forever.

~

Become large, my friend—do not remain small. Create love, Create love.
And if you cannot, then I will, as I have done in the past,
many a time, many a time.

~

You are intelligent, my friend, too intelligent.
But this does not make you alive in any way.
For you know not the language of the heart that speaks a thousand languages.
Philosophy and mathematics make not a linguist of the heart
that I wish to make of you.

~

The structure that you stand upon, which you have created for yourself,
is determined to make you believe that you will fall without it.
I will show you that it is this structure that needs you so that it may stand.

~

Tears.

I often wrote with tears in my eyes.

~

"The ship is moving swiftly ahead, and angels dance above our heads deep into the night when we cannot see but feel them. For every woman you truly love, and every woman who truly loves you, is an angel who watches over you even as you cry for her." I had a few extra cups of wine that night, after hearing The Captain's words that evening.

And I remembered the night when she had come to me in a white gown. It was no dream. It was as real as this very ship. As real.

~

What difference is there between a thing that happened in the past and a thing one dreamt of or imagined? He wondered. For they both exist only in our minds.

~

The Captain's ways were mysterious. And they flooded my mind every night, like waves on a seashore . . . one taking down another, one after the other . . . one after the other.

~

"I know you cry at night, my friends," The Captain said, looking at the ship-men. "For you live without hope aboard this ship. I know it is I who creates dreams and guarantees their demise. But these are no ordinary tears, my friends. For they carry the seeds of your eternal life within them."

The Madman was busy muttering something under his breath, but I could see The Leper's eyes welling up, for beneath the mirth he shared so generously with all was a man as ready as me to jump off this ship and take his chances with death.

The Captain did feel our pain. He did cry with us. He was no swashbuckling sailor that night. He was just a man with a plan we could not fathom no matter how much we tried. And it was he who carried the burden of all our pain . . . All our pain.

~

Who knew what words echoed as I woke up each morning . . .

Who knew where they came from,

and where they were headed . . .

~

"Wait patiently for the one," The Captain said. We were all drunk that night, but I knew it was me he was speaking to. For it was me who dreamt of a love so great . . . a love so great it would dissolve me like a grain of salt in this very sea we sailed upon. "Wait patiently, and remember that those who truly love are destined to have their hearts broken open."

~

Some days you question the very ground that you stand upon. And God gives no answers on that day. No angel visits you that night, and no captain can light the fire in your heart. You stand, like a grain of sand from a forgotten seashore, wondering . . . where it was all headed. And love . . . love was a foolish dream that would die before it could take wing. How would the dead give life to the ones yet to live? He wondered, thinking about The Captain.

~

Can you walk upon this earth, live life like a dream?
Can you die a thousand deaths today? For you have anyway, in lifetimes past.
Can you see your little ones drift away from you, even as they cling to your feet?
Can you put your hand through me and see I'm invisible now?
Can you..?

~

If a man were to see his lives already lived but forgotten... and his lives yet to be lived, would he see it as a story, with a beginning and an end... or in flashes that come to him in the middle of the night as he struggles to sleep...

~

He slapped me across my face, and I did nothing to stop him or defend myself.
"It happened," I said quietly. "It just happened."
"That is no answer, brother." He pointed his finger at me. "That is no answer."
"It's the only answer I have," I said.
"Do you not love me? Have you no respect for me?"
"She will not leave you, brother. She loves you too much. She said so."
"And why should I hear this from your mouth?" he barked.
But I had no answer.

~

"I love you and will always do. No matter what happens," she wrote to me. 'But there is nothing I can offer you, other than what I feel. We have no life together."

I tore it up, into little pieces, and threw it into the fire that blazed high on this cold winter night.

~

Deconstruct, reconstruct, deconstruct, reconstruct . . . And so it went on, till my brain could take it no more. No more.

~

God notices the ones who surrender to love.

~

"You are not special. You are just like everyone else! Who do you think you are? Have you looked in the mirror lately?" He was not known to mince His words.

I was quiet.

"Stop living with these illusions," He barked at me.

~

But no one could convince me that I wasn't special. Not even Him. I believed I was.

Undoubtedly.

From the bottom of my heart.

~

You will not have your way with love.
Love must have its way with you. It must.

~

"Find the one who loves you," He said. "She is the one for you. The one."

The one who loves me? I wondered. What about the one I love?

~

"I cannot hurt him. I love him too much," *she said, as we walked through the*
fields near the village.

"And me?" *I asked.* "You can hurt me?"

"I love him. He was my first love and will forever be my love."

I kept silent.

"You don't want to hear this, I know. But I must speak my truth."

I knew she was right. But what you most wish for in this world always survives
in the face of all reason.

Even when the truth surrounds you from every direction.

~

You are always needed, and never needed,
So be free and bound, all together. All together.

~

"This isn't going to hurt," I told myself. It had been fourteen years now. "For
you hold the idea of her, although she exists no more . . . you are in love with
a ghost."

~

And just like the ship, she vanished.

~

Dear Son,

First of all, remember that I am you and you are me.

Do you believe for a second that you cannot fly like I did? Or love as I did? Or gain the respect of my fellow men as I did?

Remember that my end was your beginning, and your life will appear to be, in many ways, the very opposite of mine. It is meant to be so.

Your mother and I created you in our image, and now you will create us in yours.

I am your father, and He is our father. And we are happy with what you have become.

There were no mistakes. Ever. Remember that when you abuse yourself, you abuse me and Him.

Do you doubt me?

Stop trying to win me. It was never needed.

Stop trying to be a man. You have been both, man and woman.

Just be.

Man keeps proving, trying. But God is tired.

Embrace yourself, as I embrace you.

Be free.

You are my son and my father, and also my brother, and my friend. You will always be a part of my heart.

Your father.

~

BOOK VI

~

The Book of Sirius

~

This is the book of Sirius, for it is the brightest star in the night sky, twice as large as the sun. Twice as large. And it is this that gives you a second birth, a new beginning that is brighter than your first. Brighter than your first.

~

I will write the book of Sirius.

~

We live our lives in blindness and cloak it with knowledge. Like a watch that keeps time but knows nothing of it.

~

*When one force gathers in strength, the opposite gains equally in strength
to counter it.*

~

*There is tremendous good in this world, even as you see, all around you,
nothing but evil. Nothing but evil.*

~

*Only when you see the insignificance of your own life will you be able to forsake
it for His. For who amongst us really wants to be the son of God?
Even though you are. Even though you are.*

~

*Your ways need not change the slightest. Not the slightest.
Just watch yourself. That is all I ask of you.*

~

*Your mind will attack, from within you and from the outside, through others.
So fight not, and yield not. Simply remain, and watch with affection its antics.*

~

You will see the world through my eyes. For it is I who lives in you.

~

I am from the day out of time. The day out of time.

~

I live for my dreams.
And I will make sure some never come to pass, so that I may live on,
so that I may live on. And have something to live for.

~

I speak to none.
I speak for you all, so that you may hear the story of your own lives
and live in remembrance.

~

I am infinitely patient as am I impatient. For time exists not, for me.

~

I make no mistakes, for this is your journey, and yours alone. Neither I nor
you can alter what is in your contract with me. For this is a sacred contract we
made a long time ago, and we swore to stay true to it.

~

Judge not another, for you know not what is in her contract. Pity not another,
for you know not what is in his contract. Embrace one and all,
for they all live by the contract, agreeably or disagreeably.

~

Like minds may share interests or thoughts. But compare not your contract
with another's. For no two contracts are alike. No two.

~

I am infinitely patient, yet I urge you not to stay in one place for too long.
I speak not of geography. Flow like a river,
always touching new shores within yourselves.

~

The value of silence is immeasurable. For not only does it nourish you, it gives
you distance to see yourself and others, so that you may embrace us all and not
go to war, as you are inclined to do.

~

I speak not of many things that are best discovered for yourselves on this jour-
ney. All I say is that what you know not is far greater than what you know.
So be humble, and pray for more knowledge that stems from the heart.
Use books to open the windows of your heart and mind,
not to enclose yourself with so-called "knowledge."

~

Fail not a single relationship, for you will fail yourself in doing so.
Find your peace instead, and embrace the other.

~

He remembered the foam on the shore. How he used to run on the soft sand that cupped his feet like old shoes.

~

You have let yourself down too many times. Too many times. Never again, you hear me, never again. The most difficult thing, yet so close to your heart, is to listen to yourself.

~

For this is a voice as soft as it is loud. As deep as it is shallow. And as cool as it is hot. It is deceptive, my friend, very deceptive. For you can judge not from where it arises.

~

Our Moment in Time

~

"It is I. I, who does everything. Not you." He heard the words as they sat that one and only day, watching the crimson-pink sunrise that bathed the skies with the rarest of colors. This was not a passing feeling, but a truth that, like the sun, came out from behind the clouds and bathed the undulating landscape till where the eyes could see.

"Love will not go unrewarded. It will not." The words resounded across the valley. "But measure not, each of you, what gift it brings. For each shall receive from it, what we decided many years ago at a time that you yourself will not remember today, but that which will be remembered in time."

"Did you hear that?" he asked her. "No," her eyes said. Why did he say that? he wondered, for he knew The Voice was in his head. "What did you hear?" she asked.

"It was about love," he replied.

"What about love?" she asked, without wanting an answer. Truly, on that day, she had no questions. She was happy to rest her shoulder on his and watch the rays of the sun slowly light up the skies.

~

And moments of togetherness like this one that had no past or future were like no other moments. They cut deep into your heart and left scars that would perhaps never go away. That was the price you had to pay for them. It was the way of life.

~

He wanted to hold her hands tight and let this moment last forever. But that was impossible, he knew. In a few minutes, once the sun shone bright in the sky, she slowly pulled her hand away from his and took a walk to sit higher up on the hill, alone. He lay down on the grass and closed his eyes, looking at the little shapes and patterns that swirled in orange and crimson.

He wondered if love was truly the greatest moment of loneliness in which you could not bear even the presence of the one who brought you to this place.

For no matter how much you wanted to be together with someone in a moment, sometimes you found yourself alone.

~

You forget now, but there was only one way your heart could be broken. Forgive me, for it was I. Not you, or her. It was I.

~

I shed a silent tear. For all the tears that had to be shed had already been shed, a long time ago.

~

Your lifetimes are mere drops in my ocean, friend. Mere drops. Like the swaying of leaves outside your window. But it is I who decides, I who decides how a leaf grows and how it falls to the earth. It is I.

~

"I speak to you, as I have spoken to so many . . . so many. I speak to you now. You cannot contain me, son, as I contain you. I contain you," he heard and cried, remembering The Captain's words. "Your tears carry the seeds of your eternal life within them. They are no ordinary tears." And he cried now for The Captain like never before, like never before.

~

And he closed his eyes and thanked the Lord for all that he had been given, and all that had been taken away from him, since the beginning of time, till this day. Till this day.

~

Be patient, son. One day I shall bequeath myself unto you. Unto you.

~

I was silent.

~

This is what you want, is it not?

To serve.

Tell me this is not true. Tell me.

~

It was true. Somewhere deep down, it was.

~

If only you knew what I knew, you would not live as you live, in strife and in terror. This is the only mission you have—to gain this sacred knowledge that must sprout from within, from within.

~

For the gravest error would be to mistake that which has been learned from outside yourself for that which must sprout from the very depths of your soul. It will do nothing but gather false pride and empty wisdom.

~

Sharpen this sword, and brandish it every day so that you may cut through the fog and cobwebs that allow you not to see life as it is.

~

When you make a choice, always call upon your higher selves.

~

Act not in haste, for haste is time wanting to slow you down. It is quiet reflection that can truly hasten your journey.

~

"Why is it you choose me?" I asked.

~

Worry not for others. And care not for your uniqueness. For the realization that all is one is far greater than whatever you could be.

~

When duty becomes your passion, you shall become one with your eternal self.

~

It is I who creates holes for you to fall in. But it is your blindness that makes you fall again and again.

~

I am the enemy of time, for I care not for rules, good or bad, or for truth, or for lies. I am the enemy of time, and I play with all elements in this sacred war.

~

I raise your past from the dead and bring your future to its knees. I count your dreams in my sleep and gift you nightmares to ponder upon.

~

You have tried winning for long enough, my friend. When will you lose? When will you truly lose?

~

How can I trust what you say? How do I know this is not my imagination?

~

Would you ask the credentials of the composer of a song that brought back the living from the dead? Would you . . .

~

I was quiet.

~

As I sat in the car and waded through the crowded traffic on the narrow lanes, I saw it.

~

They had walked to the chapel eight miles away from the village. It stood alone, grey and somber against the bright blue skies above and the green pastures below. Not a soul from the village visited this chapel, for they had their very own just half a mile away.

"Let's walk this way," he had said. "It's a beautiful path."

She agreed, and they walked a long time, silently looking at the fields and the radiant skies that were crimson pink and purple today. The chapel slowly came into view, and the moment he saw it, he knew they would be going there.

"Let us enter and make a prayer there," she said to him.

"I believe not in prayers," he replied.

"Let us enter nevertheless," she said.

Something was pulling them in. He could feel it.

~

The heavy wooden door creaked as it opened, and inside we could see the shape of a man in a cloak, kneeling in front of a row of candles.

We walked towards him quietly, not wanting to disturb. But he opened his eyes and looked at us.

"Pardon us, father. We didn't mean to disturb you," I said.

"This is the house of God, son. We are never disturbed." The priest looked upon us kindly. He was a middle-aged man, with a tall frame and soft skin.

We walked to the altar, where a statue of Jesus looked down at us. It was an old piece, imbued with love, as was the chapel, which had a warmth, unlike the one in our village.

"Will you marry me?" The words came out of my mouth. Who said these things? I wondered.

She looked at me, not fully believing what I had just said.

"Will you marry me?" I asked her again. "I ask nothing of you. Nothing. All I ask for is your hand in marriage."

"You know I am already married," she said quietly.

"That is of no consequence to me. For I seek nothing from you," I said. "Neither your company, nor your affections. All I ask is that you look inside your heart and tell me if you love me."

She was silent for a moment.

"You know I do."

"Then I wish to marry you." I could hear my own voice, firm and steady.

She said nothing. But her eyes became distant even as she looked straight into my eyes.

The priest walked towards us, smiling. "May I be of some assistance?"

"Yes, father, yes," I said.

"It is said, there is no strife when you follow the purity within your heart," he spoke, before I could say a word.

I repeated in front of the priest now. "We wish to be married, father."

"Have you run away from home?" the priest asked, looking at both of us.

"No, father. Certainly not," I replied. "This is a private matter. That is all."

The priest was quiet. As was she.

"You may marry us now, father," I said. "We follow the purity in our hearts. You can be sure of that."

And the priest began the ceremonies.

~

When it was done, I said to the priest, "Now I must make my confession, father."

He looked puzzled for a moment. Then he said, "Right here, my son. Come with me."

I walked behind him, as he led me to the confessional booth, a place I had never visited.

He took his place, and I took mine, in the dark chamber, where not a word or thought would escape God's ears.

"You promise never to speak of what I confess, father?"

"It is my oath, son. My oath to the Lord. He is all forgiving."

"Forgive me father, for I have sinned. I have sinned against God. I have sinned against my brother, and sinned against her. And for this I shall never forgive myself."

"What is your sin, my son?"

"The girl who stands there. She is my brother's wife."

~

BOOK VII

~

The Forsaken

~

Whoever said that souls are eternal and do not die? For I can say truly, I have died not once but a thousand times within a single life.

Whoever said that love sets you free? For I can say truly, it terrorizes and haunts me every single day. Every single day.

~

And I remembered the words I had written, just a few days ago.

"Judge not another, for you know not what lies in their contract. You know not."

And for a moment, peace came like a single ray of sunshine into my heart. I embraced myself exactly as I was. I could breathe.

~

When passion becomes your duty, you shall become one with your eternal self.

~

Were the opposite of all eternal truths equally true?

~

"You think you're destined for greatness, don't you?" He asked, sharply.
I said nothing. But no matter what I felt in a given moment, it never changed what I felt about myself. Never.

Was this a delusion? Or had I seen a glimpse of my future? Only time would tell, I thought to myself.

~

"It's time to row, my lads!" The Captain said, looking into the sun behind the clouds. "It's time to row. Time is running out."

We took our places, the sailsmen and the rowmen. But today, it made no difference to me whether the ship was moving or standing still.

~

All dreams of salvation are false. All hope of freedom is but a mirage.
Nothing will deliver you, my son. Not I, not anyone.
Not imaginary voices.
Not even yourself, my friend, not even yourself.

~

Why am I so arrogant?

What makes me believe that my future must seek me as much as I seek it?

What makes me believe that I need not ever find it? For it is I who must be found . . .

Something was wrong with me.

~

"Regard not your goodbyes with sadness or tears," The Captain had said to us as we began to board the ship. "Truly, they are beautiful . . . for they contain within them the seeds of reunion."

None of us had anyone to cry for or say goodbye to. We looked around, wondering whom he was speaking to. The Captain simply smiled.

And even though we knew not why he smiled, we trusted him completely. We just did.

~

These were the days when tears spontaneously fell without so much as a warning. These were the days . . .

~

Live your greatest nightmare. Live it until you are free from it. Only then can your heart rid itself of fear and experience love.

~

Live a lonely life, if that is what it is written in the books. But cloak it not. Hide it not from your heart. Experience the heart of loneliness. The very depth of it.

~

The last thing you wish for must be unattainable, for this is what leads you into your eternal self.

~

I assure you, I will break time. For it is time that holds you up so that you can stand straight and believe the things you do without so much as a doubt.

~

The cabin smelled of residual cigar smoke soaked through the years by the wooden walls. The Captain heaved as he settled into his favorite chair, the lamp above his head swinging from left to right as the faraway shouts of the sailors on the main deck could be heard in the distance.

The Leper was watching him tonight.

"You really believe in all this, don't you? You believe it. You wouldn't have it any other way, would you, you capable son-of-a-bitch? I despise you for that and that alone, sire." The Leper had drunk far too much wine, but he spoke his truth today.

The Captain smiled, but he was hardly amused.

"Belief is for fools, Leper. Those who know the truth must bear the weight of it. Either lead, or be led, I say to you," The Captain said. "Or else hold your silence in peace."

The Leper let out a small snigger as his silhouetted form emerged from behind The Captain.

"You are no different from us, Captain. No different," he said and heard his own words as he spoke. "Your arrogance will be your downfall one day."

"I fell a long time ago. A very long time ago," The Captain laughed. "Someday you, too, will have the same good fortune."

"You twist words, Captain. The truth is that we will all be dead soon enough, and the land you promise us is nothing but an excuse for your own ambitions, whatever they might be."

The Captain was not unfamiliar with accusations.

"We will all die, sire," The Leper continued. "On this floating coffin in the sea. That's what it is. One big coffin. And we are the forsaken ones . . . the forsaken . . ."

"I have heard you, Leper." The Captain was tired. "Now go back to your cabin and get some sleep, will you? You will sleep well tonight—I promise you that."

The Leper was suddenly quiet. He had never spoken to The Captain like this. He slowly ambled towards The Captain and held his hand tightly. "I am sorry, sire. Forgive me." He looked up at The Captain, his eyes glassy and teary. "I am a fool who knows not what he speaks."

"It's alright, my friend." The Captain's voice was gentle. "As I have said before to you, I will call upon your services when I need them. You have nothing to worry about. Nothing."

"Thank you, Captain, thank you," The Leper said. "I was born cursed, but you took me on this ship knowing that I would be of no good use."

"You, my friend, are of very good use. That you have no idea of this is exactly how I like it." The Captain spoke slowly. "Now go to sleep, friend. It has been a difficult day, I know. The morning shall find you in much better spirits. Go on."

The Leper slowly released The Captain's hands and walked back to his bunk in a half daze.

The Captain walked up to his bed and lay down, resting his head on his favorite pillow, listening to the faraway voices of his men, merry with wine flooding their veins. Ah, it would have been nice to have a friend these days, he thought to himself. And as always, he closed his eyes and immediately fell asleep, imagining what was to come.

~

BOOK VIII

~

The Captain's Curse

~

He had a dream that night. The Captain had walked quietly into his cabin, at a time when not a soul stirred, when not a single shipman was awake. Perhaps it was around four in the morning. He thought he heard a few birds cawing in the distance, and he could feel his heart beating faster and harder at the very thought of reaching land. It often happened to him these days. He would jump out of bed, his heart racing, believing that the ship had reached a shore.

"Wake up, lad, wake up!" The Captain shook him by his arm.

~

"Captain?" I sat up, startled.

"Yes, it is I," The Captain said, adjusting his clothes and straightening his jacket. "It is time. I must leave now."

"Where? How?" I stuttered. "You cannot leave us! And what of the ship? We will be stranded."

"Nothing to worry about, my lad, nothing to worry about. All will be well," he said, in a steady voice.

"But we know not where we are headed. It is you and you alone who can take us to land!" I cried.

"This ship sails without me, lad." He sat in a chair opposite my bunk. "You will be Captain now. I have chosen you."

"What are you saying, sire? I know not how to navigate this ship or work the sails. Besides, no one will listen to me . . ."

"This ship needs nobody, lad. I assure you it will not sink, not as long as you are in command. Take your place where you belong. You know how we came aboard this ship, and when I threw the book and told you never to share your knowledge with anyone here, you obeyed me." The Captain paused and appeared to ponder for a moment. "You are Captain now. There is no other option. No other. Take care of her, for she will lead you to freedom, to land, to love . . . everything you seek . . ."

And his voice faded.

~

He woke up to the loud creaking sounds of the ship, wondering what happened during the night. It was a bad dream, he thought to himself, as he made his way to the main deck. It was eight in the morning, and the sun was bright against a crystal-blue sky.

"Have you seen The Captain?" he asked the shipmen, trying his best not to give away the panic in his heart.

They looked at each other, shrugged, and got back to their work.

He saw The Lead Shipman and asked, "Have you seen The Captain?"

"He must be in his cabin. He was looking a bit pale last night. Coughing a lot and drinking more than his usual share of wine."

~

Only he will reach land who knows he comes from it. Only he reaches his eternal self, who knows, without a doubt, that he comes from it.

~

He ran to The Captain's cabin, with a hollow, sinking feeling in his stomach. "This ship cannot sink. This ship never reaches land. I am already dead," he remembered.

~

Nothing made sense. The Captain's cabin door was open, and there was no one inside.

"Captain!" he yelled. "Captain!" He shouted out in all directions, standing at the door.

~

But no answer came. None.

I knew The Captain had gone. Truly and surely gone. And there was no point running through the ship shouting his name when I knew the truth in my heart. Even if what I saw last night was a dream, this was certainly no dream. It was no dream.

The nightmare had begun.

~

And everything The Captain said on those wine-filled nights and every line I had read in the book—all of it rushed into me leaving me numb as I had never felt before.

~

I went to my cabin and lay down in my bunk, closing my eyes, knowing I would not sleep a deep sleep for a very long time.

~

Did he kill himself? Or was he a ghost that could disappear and appear at will?

These were the last thoughts in my head as I drifted away from the ship and from myself, wishing that I would never return.

~

BOOK IX

~

The Ship That Cannot Sink

~

"He's not here." The Lead Shipman stomped loudly into my cabin. "The Captain—where is he?"

"I don't know . . . what are you talking about?" I said, unconvincingly, as I lay on my bed, opening my eyes just enough to see him.

"You were asking for him earlier this morning." His voice was unwavering. "Why?"

"I don't know . . . he didn't say." I closed my eyes again, turning away from him.

"You know something." He grabbed my hand and sat me up. "What is it?"

The Madman walked behind him, saying, "The Captain's gone! He's gone!"

"He said nothing," I said quietly.

"He must have said something," The Lead Shipman said, wanting an answer that I did not want to give.

"It was in a dream. How can I say . . ."

"What dream?"

~

Everything I did was to create you. Everything I did was for you.

~

"I cannot do it. I cannot do this job," I said.

He was quiet. "So you accept your inability?"

"Yes," I said, after a moment's silence.

"Why don't you also accept your incapability in your personal life?" He asked.

"I do," I said, but I knew I didn't really mean that. Whenever I spoke to Him, I knew exactly when I was lying.

~

"He walked into my room, in my dream, and told me things." I paused. "But it was a dream. It wasn't real."

"How are you sure it was a dream?"

"Because I know. I just know. I dream of many things—you know that. I dream all the time."

"But you were the first to know about The Captain's disappearance." The Lead Shipman was no fool. "Whatever he told you in your dream must be true."

"He said he was leaving. That's all he said."

"That cannot be. I know The Captain. It cannot be." His voice rose again. "You are hiding something, lad. I know my Captain. I know him better than all of you. And I know he said more than what you are telling me. Why do you lie, friend? Why?"

"Because what he said cannot be true! It cannot!" I stood up and said. "It was a dream. Just a dream."

"But what did he say?" He was insistent.

"He said I was The Captain now. And the ship would not sink as long as it was in my command."

The Lead Shipman was silent for more than a few moments. He instantly remembered his conversation with The Captain yesterday night at the lower deck.

~

White is the color of death, not black. For when you pass through this door, you will come out clean of everything.

~

"I fear for this ship. I fear for her." The Captain had rambled as he gulped his eleventh cup of wine.

"But why, Captain?" The Lead Shipman asked. "We have faith in you. I have faith in you. And that is all that matters."

"This ship is in danger of sinking. I can sense it. And it is with a heavy heart that I say I cannot do a thing about it." The Captain's eyes were red.

"Time is running out," The Captain mumbled. "Time is running out."

"What can we do, then?" he asked The Captain. "Guide us."

"Nothing ever repeats . . . Nothing lasts forever . . ." The Captain continued mumbling.

"What can we do, sire? Please tell us."

"You know nothing, friend, nothing," he rambled on. "For you remember nothing. Fools—that's what you all are . . . fools."

The Lead Shipman's face fell. The Captain's words hit him across his face in a way that not even the most ferocious storms did in the middle of the rains. His head was down now.

"But only you can save this ship, Shipman—only you," The Captain continued. "For you have faith in me like none on this ship."

"Yes, sire," he said quietly, lifting his head up a little.

Something was strange about this conversation, The Lead Shipman thought.

~

"I cannot be Captain of this ship. If anyone at all should be Captain, it should be you," I said.

"I follow the orders of The Captain, lad," he said firmly, without hesitation. "If he has told you that you are Captain, then you are."

"It was a dream, I tell you. Just a dream," I repeated.

"Perhaps. But you were the first to know, and that makes your dream as real as the land that we sail towards. Now get yourself ready, and take your place on the front deck." He was calm now. "It was my promise to The Captain, a long time ago, that, as long as I am alive, I will ensure this ship does not sink."

I was relieved to hear these words. For I knew we were not immortal. I knew we could drown in the sea. And I knew that The Captain's ways were not to be trusted anymore.

I was alone now.

~

Remember The Captain's words. Remember all that you can remember.
And all that you do not want to remember.

~

A Walk by the River

~

Like the deep, dark sea,
You pull me in.
Until I cannot breathe,
Until I cannot see,
Until I cannot taste the salt in the water,
Until all that's left of me,
Is a single breath that
struggles to keep me alive.
The single breath
that I took centuries ago
when I kissed you.

~

When pain is your greatest friend,
Death becomes your ultimate wish.

~

He woke up to the uneasy swaying of the ship. It was not the season for storms and raging seas, but today, the sounds he usually heard at night felt loud and dangerous. Should he reveal to the others what he knew, now that The Captain was no longer there? "All in good time . . . All in good time," he could hear The Captain's voice saying, and if he knew one thing, just one thing, then it was this—listen to The Captain at all times, especially now.

~

He remembered the day when The Captain had saved his life with his unshakeable grip. He could do none of those things. None. Not even drink wine and make merry with the shipmen, who, it seemed, had accepted The Captain's sudden departure with unexpected ease. The ship had slowed a little. But The Lead Shipman ensured the good cheer of the shipmen. And so, it sailed on steadily, just as The Captain had said it would.

~

You will start with a wish in your heart. Slowly, it turns into a dream, a hope.
It turns into a deep belief when there is no proof
of your dream ever coming true.
Trust is what is left when there is proof that your dream will never come true.

~

He had traveled as far north as he could. But there was no magical forest and no sages with mystical powers to be found. It was like any other forest, filled with trees of all shapes and sizes, with creepers growing all over them. And the sun's rays filtered in through the gaps and reached the bushes and shrubs down below. Not a soul was there to be found. Not a soul. He strode through the bushes using a stick to clear the way forward, eating a fruit or two that he could recognize and walked on, hoping for something. Anything.

He climbed the rocky and dense region and steadily made his way to the top of the hill that looked closer than it was. As he reached the top, he could see all *the way down, the river cutting through the valley like an old, curved silver knife, glimmering from the light of the sky.*

~

The ship was slowly but surely weakening. The sails were in tatters, and the constant repair the ship needed was sparingly done. The Lead Shipman could attend to only so much.

The shipmen mumbled and spoke among themselves. But gradually they became quiet. They had to accept their fate. The Madman laughed. "The Captain's gone. He vanished. I knew it. I knew it."

The Leper was quiet. He had no one to question now. No one to doubt. No one to follow. And no one to despise. The Lute Player was hardly a Captain. And he was his friend to boot.

There was no left one to blame.

~

He walked downwards, through the forest, carefully watching his step, and in the distance he could now hear the gentle sound of water. As he approached the river, his heart was full of that sound, and he rushed towards the waters, with his stick in his hand. It was as if the most beautiful thing in this world was waiting for him. For the river that he could now clearly hear was the only moving thing in this loneliest of forests.

~

A man who surrenders seeks no pleasures. Pleasures seek him now.

~

He would wake up in the middle of the night these days, as if possessed. He could see her lips, her long brown hair, and her eyes. He could touch them. He could feel them. It was no dream, and it was no nightmare. It was his memory, perhaps from the future, returning to him.

How much he wanted her now. How much. He closed his eyes and imagined holding her in his arms, with her head close to his chest. It was the opposite of everything he saw on this ship, which was rusting and rotting away right in front of his eyes. As he put his head down, he felt every single long and endless night ahead of him. And time appeared to have forsaken him all over again.

~

He reached the river, and, as if for the first time in his entire existence, cupped the water with his dry hands, drinking the clear water that swirled and danced against the round pebbles below. He placed his clothes on a flat rock and walked in slowly, naked, feeling the cool water rise from his feet to his legs and then to his torso. With his hands cupped together, he took the water and raised it above his head, as if raising a toast to this moment. Or making an offering to the gods for what he felt today.

After many months or years—he couldn't tell—a sense of bliss surged through every cell in his body. In that sacred moment, the cool waters washed away the struggle and the pain that he had carried till now. The pain of trying to forget a life that wasn't even lived and the pain of remembering a life that he wished to forget.

~

The Fall from Grace

~

The day you realize every moment is truly miraculous,
miracles truly begin to happen.

~

You fell from grace, I know, my son. You fell so greatly that now you wish
never to rise again. Never again. But it was I, my son.
I raised you, and I made you fall.
And it is I who shall make you rise once again. Once again. And it is I who
will make you fall, if I so wish. Surrender to me. Surrender.

~

He could see the sun's reflection glittering through the water as it left his hands and fell into the river. He could taste the smell of the fresh water that was infused with beauty and love as it caressed his body. He took a deep breath and dived in, opening his eyes inside the river where existed another world nothing like his own. It was peaceful and silent, and yet alive with life. What a beautiful thing water was! Without form and without color, and yet so close to the very essence of life. For without water, no life could exist.

He swam for a while, his muscles gathering strength as they moved against the current of the river, and came back to the bank where his clothes lay.

~

As I write, grace descends, and layers of myself are shed. The spirit shines forth in all its radiance. I am absent, and the Lord is all that exists. "Yes! It's true. It's true," The Voice says. And the drums beat, and the invisible music plays on endlessly, like stars shining in the sky, whether we see them or not.

~

Not knowing what else to do, he followed the river, for the river became his best friend and companion. It moved east, towards the morning sun, he knew, as he walked along the riverside. He would sleep under the trees, and even though the sound of the forest was loud with the sound of insects and the earth was hard beneath his body, he slept dreamlessly and restfully. Perhaps it was gifted to him these days. For he had slept many a night with cool winds blowing and a warm blanket, but a restful sleep rarely came to him.

~

The greatest error is to forget the very reason
for what you chose once upon a time.

~

It was six months after the wedding that he had gone to her room, with a cup of chicken broth. She was running a fever for the third day now, and his brother was away on work. She lay there in bed, shivering and pale. Yet he found her as beautiful as he did on the day of the wedding, laughing and dancing. He helped her to sit up.

"Take this. You will gain in strength."

"I can try. But the sight of food nauseates me," she replied.

He put his hand on her neck. It was burning. He wished for a moment that he could take away her fever and bring it into his own body. He knew that it was impossible. Still, he wished it with all his heart.

He brought some cool water and, with a soft cloth, pressed her forehead like his mother did when he was a child. Time stood still as he continued till late into the night. Why did he feel this outpouring of love? Why did he feel that the person he was looking at was his own . . . that she was his very own.

"Thank you, for everything," she said, with her eyes half-open.

"I love you," he said.

She smiled weakly and held his hand for a moment, realizing, despite her state, how much he meant what he had just said to her.

She was no fool. Not in the least.

~

Imagine days without a purpose. You long for them. You make your plans around them. You toil and sweat all your life so that you can earn them. And yet, when I gift you this never-ending journey, you cry for a destination.

~

Cherish these days. Cherish these days. For these are the happiest days of your life, I promise you.
Cherish these days. For soon, the infinite burden of the world shall be upon you.

~

The Smell of Fear

~

This watching I speak of, you will know of it when the sea of seas comes to your doorstep. It is my gift to you.

~

You are my vessel. For even though you cannot contain me, you will have to.

~

We sat around the table the following day, The Lead Shipman, The Leper, The Winemaker, and I, sipping on the same broth that was made every day.

"I propose that The Lead Shipman take over the ship. He is best qualified to do it," The Leper said, looking from side to side as he always did.

I said nothing.

"The Captain's orders must be followed at all costs," The Lead Shipman said.

"But we know not of The Captain's orders," The Winemaker added. "Why did The Captain not tell us all?"

"He told me the night before he left," The Lead Shipman said. "That is enough for you all." It was the very first time a lie had escaped his lips. For the one thing he was not was a liar. It was his pride and his honor, above all, that truth must be told at all costs.

I looked at him, shocked at what he had just said.

"I fear for this ship," The Winemaker said, in his deep but now somber voice. It was the first time I saw a hint of despair in his usually twinkling eyes and cheerful face.

"I hear The Captain's voice. I hear it." Only The Madman remained his usual self. In fact, he was more cheerful than he had ever been. "All is well, my friends. This ship is safe. So fear not ye who dares to sail this anchorless and Captain-less boat. The promised land is close, I promise you. But your end is near." He laughed, grabbing his own throat with his large knotty hands and making the sound of a man drowning in the waters.

"Pay no attention to him," The Lead Shipman said. "I believe The Captain still guides this ship. I believe so."

"You sound no more sane than The Madman here," The Leper cried. "The Captain has abandoned us! This is the truth!"

"I will not hear you speak of The Captain like this. It is you who is the fool!" The Lead Shipman was angry. "Do you wish to take charge of this ship? All you do is come forth with your questions. You have not a single answer! You never have."

"But neither do you, sire." The Leper spoke with a bitter but even tone now. "And even if The Captain did know, he would not say so. And now we are the ones who suffer for it."

The Leper hobbled way. And The Winemaker followed him slowly.

My heart was racing. But not a word came out of my mouth.

The Lead Shipman looked at me and asked, "What was in that book that made you dive into the very depths of this great ocean? Why cannot you tell me?"

~

I said nothing—not because I didn't want to, but because The Captain had told me not to.

~

BOOK X

~

The Wall of Water

~

He walked for many days . . . each day filled with a magical purity that,
despite the rocky terrain and the icy-cold breeze that sometimes passed through
the valley, never dimmed. And for the first time in his life, there was nothing he
wanted more than what was there already. The days of wanting were a distant
memory. As if they belonged to a different person. For though he had no future,
he was also free from his past. Still he walked along the river with a sense of
purpose. As if where he was headed was exactly where he was supposed to go,
even though there was truly nothing he sought.

~

What looks like a miracle is
Sometimes the illusion.
Are you listening?
What looks like a miracle is

102

Sometimes the illusion.

And what looks like the illusion

Is sometimes the miracle.

Open your eyes. Learn to see.

Learn to see.

~

I was silent today. And not a sound came from the deep, dark valley of the city lights that lay before me. Yet in its silence, much was heard. For the silence of God can sometimes be deafening.

I wanted an answer. But answers needed words. And this was not the order of the day.

~

I woke up the next morning with a jolt. My jaw was tight and my head heavy, as if a thousand lives had been lived that night.

~

I allow you, my Lord and Master, to take over.

I have failed. Utterly.

~

Meanwhile a storm was brewing. A thousand birds flew over our ship, squawking as they passed the dark grey clouds above us. Rains lashed at the ship, and the hull creaked and grunted like an old woman. The shipmen took their places at the deck and the hull, but this time there were no songs, no loud voices, and no clanging of the large bell on the upper deck that usually signaled the coming of a storm. The urgency and excitement were replaced by silent action. After all, this was the first storm they were facing without The Captain, and it was no small one at that. Even The Winemaker, who usually stayed below and waited out the storms, took a place on the deck.

"This is no ordinary storm," The Lead Shipman said to me as we stood on the top of the deck and looked through the old telescope. "The Captain had warned me about this. He feared for this ship."

"But even so . . . The Captain cannot be wrong. He is never wrong," I said, remembering The Captain's words: "As long as you are Captain of this ship, it cannot sink."

"This ship cannot sink, my friend. It cannot," I heard myself say. "I will stand at the front of the deck. Go quickly, and instruct the rowmen down below of what they must do. Then return to your sails."

A surge of energy pulsed through my body. Even though I was consumed with fear. "I must be The Captain of this ship. Dream or not, it is all I have."

"It is all we have . . ." he said, turning away and walking towards the lower deck.

~

"And one more thing . . ." I shouted in his direction.

"Yes, sire," he joked, with a broad smile on his face.

"Thank you, my friend. Thank you for having faith in me."

"I have faith in The Captain."

"You wanted to know what was in the book," I said.

"Yes." His voice was clear.

"It was our story . . . my story."

"I do not understand."

"We boarded this ship many years ago, somewhere off a coast on the Celtic sea. It has been fourteen years now."

"How do you know this for sure?"

"Because I remember it clear as day," I said. "The book was from the future. And it knew of everything."

He was silent.

"I know how we got here. I know many things," I continued. "Except where we are headed. That, only The Captain knows." The sound of thunder broke above in the skies. The Lead Shipman listened carefully.

"But you are Captain now. So you will know that soon enough," he said.

"For all our sakes, I hope I do," I said.

"Just trust yourself. Trust your Captain."

But trust was a feeling farthest away from myself. I trusted nothing, least of all myself.

— ~

You want to ask a thousand questions. But not even one escapes your lips.

You want to tear yourself from where you are. But instead you stay still, like a leaf on a branch.

You want to cry a stream of tears, but instead you smile quietly and wait for it to turn real.

You want to end this throttling existence, but The Voice says, "It is you that has to end. Existence is free. You are bound."

And you try your very best to take it in.

~

As he made his way along the rapids and the jagged rocks that now broke the river's smooth flow, he could hear the sound of the water falling and hitting the riverbed down below with a roar. He kept to the side, slowly moving over the rocks, holding on to the branches for safety. As he got closer, the roar got louder and louder until he could hear nothing else. It was a beautiful sight. The entire breadth of the water cascaded and fell far down below, as far as his eyes could see. Mist rose towards the skies, and the tiny drops kissed his face like a soft cloud. The earth was moist, and the skies were damp and overcast. He walked away from the waters, trying to find his way down below. It was evening now, and the light was slowly fading. He found a path around the waterfall and reached the smooth terrain that was down below. The sun had set, but it was a full-moon night, full of promise and full of a silvery light that had turned the landscape into an unimaginably beautiful sight.

~

He stood at the front of the deck as he had seen The Captain stand not long ago, and he looked ahead to see how long it would be before the storm hit the ship. Not more than ten minutes, he thought to himself.

"It's a big one!" The Madman shouted, his large hands tightly holding the mast. "Never seen anything like it!"

And as the moments passed, it was clear that what was coming would certainly bring the ship down. For what was approaching fast was no storm but a wave that was three times the size of the ship. It was a wall of water that was closing in.

"My friends, hear me now!" I said, loud and clear for all to hear. "If you want to live, my shipmen, you must be ready to die. Only those ready to die will live to see land, or eternity, whatever it is you wish to see. So let us test the gods today instead and show them not that we are strong enough to live but that we are afraid not to die. I will walk with you, my friends, through this valley of death. I will sink to the bottom of this ocean with you, my friends. For this wave is no ordinary wave. It is the sea of seas that now approaches us. We are but specks of sand on this earth. So fear not this dark passage that appears to mark your end. Fear it not."

He listened to what he had just said, once again, as if someone else had spoken the words. The shipmen raised their hands and cheered. He yelled out to The Lead Shipman, "We will sail this ship headlong into the wave. So turn your masts to the north, and fill your sails with the wind from the southeast."

"Are you sure of this?" he asked me.

"What we cannot avoid, we must face head on," I replied. "There is no better way." I continued listening to myself speak.

"All masts into the wind!" The Lead Shipman shouted.

And soon enough, the ship was heading straight into the wave.

~

What if I had to give you something you could not imagine wanting? Something that was impossible to wish for . . .

~

What are you doing, Captain? What are you doing? I screamed to him in my head. This ship is going to go down, Captain. It is sinking, this ship that never sinks. This ship that never sinks . . . is sinking.

And tears streamed down my face as he saw the wall of water coming swiftly towards the ship.

~

And as it touched the ship, the first man it took was him . . . me. The waters touched his face, and in a fraction of a moment, I was set free from the ship.

~

The waters swirled and gushed around me. This was when eternity and a single moment came together, for I could not tell if it lasted an entire lifetime or passed in no time at all. But all was well. All of a sudden, my hands and legs were free. And my lungs were light as they had ever been. Suddenly, I was alone. Was I dead? Or alive? I was in the very heart of the ocean, neither struggling for life nor afraid of death. And it felt like love was already lived. Already lived.

~

Day One

~

"It is customary for you all to have a cup of wine before you board the ship," The Captain had said, proudly holding his cup high in the air and taking a swig. "This wine will not only warm your tormented souls, it shall make you new again. For whatever burdens you carry with you, it will burn them away and make you innocent again. So have a cup or two, my lads, perhaps more. Because the more you drink, the lighter you shall feel. This is no time to be modest or to use good judgment. For good judgment has already led you to this ship, and it is now time to throw it to the wind and the seas that we shall sail upon for a long, long time . . ."

And as we sipped and quaffed the sweetest of wines, our minds and hearts became empty, and we entered the ship in a drunken stupor, never to remember our old lives again. Or how we came aboard.

~

And from that day onwards, we were on this ship since eternity.

~

The next morning, we woke up, a little dazed, and slowly climbed to the upper deck, where The Captain stood smiling and looking as fresh as the night before. "Hear me carefully, my lads. For what I say is more important than you will ever know."

He spoke from the front deck, and all the shipmen could see him clearly. In his one hand was a cigar, and in the other, an emerald-green cup that looked as old as it was beautiful.

"You know not why you are here, I know. But trust me, my lads, I shall take you to the promised land that you know deep in your heart exists. I lie not to you, I promise. I lie not. So find your places and breathe in deep the smell of the sea. For this shall be your home for a day or a lifetime, I know not which. This is your journey, my friends. So work hard on the task you will be given, and above all, carry hope in your heart for that which your heart truly seeks. That is all I can say now. That is all." He paused for a moment and spoke again. "If you know not what your heart truly desires, then pray that you find it on this ship, for whatever can be found will be found on this very ship, my friends. On this very ship."

And he slowly descended down the staircase that led to the main deck, where I stood, half drunk from last night. This cannot be real, I told myself. It could not.

I stood at the side, staring into the infinite seas all around me. How long have I been here? I wondered.

~

"Welcome aboard, son." The Captain stood next to me and spoke in his deep voice. "The sea is beautiful, isn't it? I can watch it for hours, even days. And time can hardly keep up with me when I do, for days, even months, can pass at a moment's notice."

"Yes, sire," I replied.

"Do you play the lute?" he asked.

"No, sire."

"I have an old one that my Captain gave me when I came aboard his ship. Perhaps you would enjoy playing a tune or two," he smiled and said.

"I could try, sire," I said.

"Love songs, perhaps," he continued.

I found myself blushing. "I know nothing of love, sire. I am ignorant in these matters."

"Never touched a woman in your life?" He smiled again.

I thought hard, but nothing quite came to mind. "Perhaps not, sire."

"Ah, you have much to look forward to, my lad. When you have the time, go down to the lower deck, near the wine casks. There are trunks full of love stories. Full of love stories. They will give you hope. And it is hope on which this ship sails forth."

"Yes, sire," I said, nodding my head, but he had already left.

I saw The Leper looking on from above, hanging on to the mainsail that extended from one side of the ship to the other. He grinned and slowly came down to where I stood.

~

"Looks like The Captain's taken a liking to you, boy," he chuckled. "Giving you his lute and all." We walked towards the main deck, where the rest of the men stood talking and hustling.

"Perhaps," I replied. "That is not for me to say."

"So you've never touched a woman, eh?" He chuckled again.

I was embarrassed. "I suppose not."

"Don't fret, boy. Neither have I!" He laughed under his breath. "At least not one that I didn't have to pay afterwards." He laughed again.

I smiled.

"I like you, lad. You're a good soul, you are. I can see why The Captain likes you, too. I can see." He walked away, enjoying his hobble that day, for the very first time *in his life. He liked it here. He didn't quite know why, but he did. He felt purposeful. He was a shipman, after all . . . something he never imagined he would ever be.*

~

I will be used, my friend. I will be used . . . for there is too much love between us for you to doubt me.

~

Used for what? I wondered.

~

The waters were steady now, and he floated inside the bottom of the ocean. It was the most beautiful sound he had ever heard, a continuous, soundless hum that could not be described in any way. And before he could ask the question, he heard the answer: 'It is I that keeps you alive . . . What do you want?

You are.

To be free. From everything.

~

It was all happening together, in that same moment.

The answers came, just a moment before the question could be asked.

~

Believe it.

I cannot believe it.

You will know.
How will I know?

There is no need to know.
I don't know.

There is no "how" when you are out of time.
But how?

Are you really?
But I feel the same.

Stay quiet.
I cannot take it.

Yes.
I know nothing.

Perfect.
I know nothing.

~

The summer sun was beating down on the orchards. We had toiled hard during the year, and the grape buds had broken in spring and flowered early summer. But this season, the flowers did not seed as they should. Most of them fell off the plants, and whichever few did mature were destroyed by the rains that fell during the last part of fruiting. It was the wrong time for the rains, and what they did was destroy whatever was left of the grapes that were fit for harvesting.

When I went to sleep that night, I wondered what sort of King allowed his own crops to die. He was no ordinary King. He had to have known better. He had to.

~

You have complete faith, my friends, that nothing will change.
I have complete faith that everything already has.

~

"The promised land, my friend, is within you.
I never lied to you, my friend. I never lied."
I heard The Captain's voice.

~

"We will have sacks of gold coins, more than you can ever imagine," He had said, to all of us who worked all day and hardly slept at night. "We will live in castles, sleep on silk and satin, and drink all day without a care in this world. We will, my friends, we will."

~

But today, in the middle of the sea, I heard what I had never heard before.
"I speak to the businessmen in all of you. The ones seeking profit and gain. The ones seeking the promised land that will never deliver you. The promised land that this whole world runs after. I speak to you all... The ones who believe it lies outside of you."

~

Remember why you boarded this ship. Remember.
Remember who I am. And you shall know what you are.

~

I say nothing different. I repeat the same thing, again and again, till I am myself deaf with it.

Entire crops. Entire crops.

~

And he knew not whether the sea had taken him in or he had jumped a moment before.

~

I can sink this ship, too, my friend, if that is what has to be done.

~

BOOK XI

~

The Divine Flaw

~

Yes.

I think I love her. I still do.

~

Yes.

And I love all the good things in life.

~

Perfect.

I hate the heat.

115

~

Great.

I love good alcohol and good food.

~

Sure.

I want to spend money. Lots of money.

~

Everything is allowed.

Is everything allowed?

~

Do not hurt anyone. That is the only condition.

It cannot be.

~

Yes.

That's a discussion for another time.

~

What is it your heart says?

What else?

~

I speak from you.

Who am I speaking to?

~

I was always you.

Who are you?

~

You cannot speak to that which speaks through you.

How can I speak to God?

~

See it.

I don't feel that.

~

You did not betray him. And he did not betray you.
All promises are kept forever.

~

"You arrogant bastard!" The Crazy One said. "You think you will understand your way to freedom, to your eternal self? Your mind is nothing. Your mind knows nothing!"

I wanted to get up and walk right out of the door. But that had been done many times before. Many times.

"It is love that changes everything. Not intelligence. Not understanding. It is love," she said to me, raising her finger towards me. She really was crazy.

I felt anger rushing into my heart.

"You think your intelligence will lead you to freedom?" She laughed. "You need tremendous love in your heart. The kind of which you have not felt till now."

"I DON'T have love in my heart," I yelled back. "There's nothing here. You don't understand. Nothing!" I beat my hand against my chest. "I feel no love. Not for anyone. Nothing at all. NOTHING."

"I know, I know," she said, gently now. "It's empty. It has to be. But it will return."

"I'm not arrogant," I said. My voice sounded like a child's. Like when I was ten. "He forgot me. He forgot all about me."

"He never forgot," she said, putting her hand around my head and holding it. "How could He . . . You are His . . . son."

"I let Him down."

~

The Day I Would Never Forget

~

You came as a boy. You became a man. I made you a child.
Now you are all.

~

"Listen to everyone as if they are God's last words," The Crazy One said. "He speaks from everywhere. Everywhere."

I had heard this before. I had. Something like this.

~

Get ready to fall in your own eyes. That's when you will truly succeed.

~

"I told you I would die for you, my love. I told you." I heard my own voice as my body spun in the middle of the salty waters. "But now I am just dying, my love. For nothing . . . For nothing . . ."

~

The Ant and Me

~

I saw him, slowly crawling up to the side of the plate, filled with lucent red pomegranate grains. And my finger went to crush him. I didn't want ants eating out of my plate.

But right before I crushed him, my hand froze. How could I kill something so weak, so delicate and so harmless? Was my life more significant than his? How was he to know that this was my plate of fruit? How far would I go to keep what I believed was mine?

~

I felt a wave of revulsion towards myself. And it wasn't just hate or disgust. It was much deep than that. Much deeper.

In fact, there was no word for that in the English language. None that I could think of.

~

Why was I feeling these things? What was happening to me?

~

Die, my beloved, die.

Don't struggle so much.

I am with you.

I am with you.

I will not kill you, my friend.

But I will watch you die and die with you.

I will.

~

It was then that I saw The Madman, inside the middle of the sea. His large hands and feet moving steadily, as if to a gentle rhythm.

"You're not crazy, are you . . ." I said.

"You do know that a 'yes' or a 'no' would mean the exact opposite," he said, smiling.

I couldn't follow.

"A 'yes' would mean I am aware and therefore sane," he explained. "And a 'no' would mean I believe my world to be completely real. You understand?"

I smiled back. "I could never understand you. Only sometimes, in bits and parts."

"I never understood myself, either," he replied. "That has not changed."

"Then what has?" I asked.

"One can listen without understanding . . . Just listen," he replied. "Sometimes it works better."

"Do you understand yourself now?"

"What is there to understand?" He smiled. "I listen, as it is not me who speaks. It is him. Him. The Captain."

"And what does he say to me now?"

"Why did you really come aboard this ship? Why?"

"Freedom? Love?" I asked. "I don't really know."

"Of course, you do. Even if you cannot say it in words."

I said nothing.

"Well, then, who are you?" he asked. "You must know who you are . . ."

"I never thought of it."

~

"Am I crazy, too, like you?" I asked The Madman.

"Isn't anyone who came aboard the ship?" he replied.

I smiled.

"You like defining things, don't you?" he said. "Constantly. Even though you know nothing."

He was right.

"Give up your reason, your logic," he continued. "Lawyers on both sides argue for their truth. But both walk away empty-handed."

I listened.

"Join me. I will take you on a journey unimaginable," he smiled and said.

What was I doing? I had already failed The Captain. And here in the middle of the ocean, I had to decide whether I wanted to live or die. Follow The Madman, or go back to the surface.

~

He called that very instant.

"Where are you?" He asked.

"I'm here, at home." I replied. But I knew I was far away. Everything felt like a dream. Even His voice, which was usually clear and firm, echoed.

What was real? What was this spiritual journey I had decided to take? And who was He really? Was He even real? Was I projecting things onto Him? Where had I brought myself? Where was I going? The confusion was so intense that my head hurt.

"OK—chill . . ." He said, as if He had heard all the things that were going through my head. "I will talk to you tomorrow."

~

Speak to me, Captain, speak to me . . . Say something . . . I cried in my heart. But it was all quiet.

~

Of course, it was. For I knew that when you are most desperate for an answer is when you least get it.

~

"What are you waiting for?" The Madman said.

"The ship. What happened to the ship? The others . . . Can I still go back?"

"The ship was for you," he replied. "Stop holding on to it. It has released you."

"But the others . . . do they still sail?" I asked.

"Release the ship, my friend," he answered. "For it has released you. Release the ship."

~

The Words I Never Heard

~

"There are no rules here. We make them up as we go along . . ." The Madman had said once, from the top of the mast.

But the winds were strong that day, and I could barely hear what he said.

"And one more thing. Be careful . . ." he continued. But the wind ate up the words before they could reach me.

"What?" I yelled back, looking in his direction

But he said nothing.

~

"What did you say?" I asked him when he came down. "I could not hear you."

"Nothing," he replied quietly. "Nothing."

But I knew it was something. Something important.

~

Sometimes you're not quite ready to hear the truth. Even if that was exactly what was needed . . .

~

It was a bright, full-moon night, and after many a cup of wine, The Leper and I jumped off the ship in the middle of the night, playing with death in the cold seawater that made us both feel alive like we had never felt before. We swam like fish, taking in the sounds of the night and the silver light of the moon. The Leper moved slowly, despite his hardened limbs. But he was equally at ease with the water. "He promised me that I would be his most trustworthy comrade one day," he said. *"I don't know when that day will come. But it will—I am sure of that."*

The Leper rarely spoke from his heart. I heard his words. But I was too happy that night to remember what he had said. After all, what doesn't stick was never really heard.

~

And another night, when we had danced all night on the upper deck, years ago, on the first day of spring, The Leper had said to me after many a wine, "I love him and hate him, all at once. It is my curse." But those days I loved The Captain too much to understand what he meant. And what you cannot understand is never really heard.

~

"It could be your blessing," I told The Leper today, silently in my mind, wondering if he'd heard my words. For I knew today that anything could be spoken or heard at any point in time. By anyone. Anywhere.

~

"I am tired, my friend," The Winemaker had said to me one day, soon after I had discovered the book. "I need something to believe in. This world has given me everything it can, but what I really want to understand is this universe and how it really works. I want to know the mind of God."

We stood at the side of the deck and stared at the infinite sea. I saw him, like a bewildered child, both lost and in awe of a greater force that he could feel but never fathom.

I wasn't interested in the universe. All I could think about was the touch of a woman I had only recently found in my future. I would meet her one day. I would.

~

"Be patient. Be patient," I wanted to tell The Winemaker. No wish goes unheard. At least not the ones that spring from the bottom of one's heart . . .

And even if he got no answer from me on that day, I'm sure he heard something today. Perhaps as a whisper in his ear, or in a dream . . .

~

The Madman was the sanest of them all. He was a shrewd trader who knew better than to board a ship with a Captain that looked crazy, with his cup of wine and his odd jacket, walking around with a pompous arrogance that was without achievement or reason.

"What's in it for me, Captain?" he had asked before he boarded the ship.

"Nothing," The Captain had replied. "Tell me: what is it that you lack, my friend?"

"Nothing."

"If that is so, then what makes you go crazy?" The Captain asked.

"Nothing. Absolutely nothing," he replied.

125

"Hmm . . . Well, first of all, I must insist you drink a cup of our oldest wine. It could be the finest you ever tasted."

"If you insist," he replied.

"I certainly do," The Captain said, pouring a cup for him and staring at him as he finished the cup in a single gulp.

"You have a big appetite, don't you, my friend?" The Captain said, pouring him another cup.

"I guess so," he replied, before he gulped that one, too, with one quaff.

"Then madness shall be your gift from today!" The Captain laughed. "They say the mad cannot distinguish between what is real and what goes on in their head. It's all the same to them."

"Is that so?" The Madman asked, before he walked onto the ship slowly, wondering why he had decided to leave his trade early that night to take a walk down to the port for some fresh air.

~

The mad were also arrogant in their own way . . . They believed they were special. Perhaps it was because they were actually frightened . . . frightened of their ordinariness.

~

"He is the One," The Strange One had said to me, after she first met Him, more than fifteen years ago. "I will walk with Him wherever He goes."
She's strange, I thought to myself. But who was He? I wondered, for never had she spoken like this about anyone till now. Never.
"He is the One," she said again. But I couldn't understand her then.

~

"Don't enter so deep, my friend. You'll not be able to come out," He had said, when He found out I was in love.

I nodded. But truly I didn't hear that. Neither did I want to.

Even if it was told to me a thousand times.

~

"Remember, fourteen years ago, we were walking on MG road, in Bangalore, and you said to me, 'Let's change this world,'" He said to me, as if reminiscing.

"Yes, I do," I replied.

"Don't forget that," He said. "Don't forget that." And He hung up the phone.

~

What I didn't hear that day, fourteen years ago, was The Voice which had laughed, "First fix yourself. Then worry about the world."

I heard it today.

~

Be ordinary. Let go of the idea that you need nothing
You need everything. You need everyone. Be free now to be what you want.
But be humble in your ways. Be silent. And make no haste,
for this is the time for flowering, not plucking flowers from the plants
that are in bloom or making offerings of them.

~

I didn't fully understand all of this.

~

"Every relationship is important. Make all your relationships complete. Treat everyone like family," He had said to me several times over the years.

But it never really went in. I was much too concerned with myself.

~

"I love you very much," she had said, as I shut the door behind me.

But I didn't hear that. I was in too much of a rush to leave everything behind.

All I heard was, "You'll be back."

The last three words I wanted to hear.

And she had cried all night for her son that day and many other days henceforth. The son who perhaps would never return. He was slowly beginning to look exactly like his father—the way he ate, the way he walked—he was, after all, a living fragment of the man who had given her everything and much more than she could have ever imagined: a love that was full of joy and a life that felt like a distant dream now.

~

"Let go. Let go," The Voice had said. "How far can he go from those who love him and those he loves? He will return. He will." But she heard only the first few words, "Let go. Let go." The fear of losing him was too great to hear anything else. And life had already taught her that things could be taken away from you in an instant—like the day her husband left in the morning to fetch wood from the

forest and never returned. There was a forest fire, they had said. Everything was charred to the ground. Nothing remained.

The only thing left to live for were her three children—her two daughters and her three-year old son, who within a few weeks smiled and laughed like nothing had ever happened. Like he had never even had a father. After all, it was impossible to miss someone you had completely forgotten.

~

I stood on the terrace of my apartment in Delhi, having a cup of tea, enjoying my last few days in the city. Whether I had lived in this home, in this city, for a year or a decade, I could not tell.

But it was time to pack my bags and move to the next city I was assigned to work in—Mumbai.

~

Now there is no place that you will ever truly leave.
And no place that you will not feel as your home.
No place.

~

I closed my eyes and took a deep breath.

~

May 15, 2013

BOOK XII

~

The Forgotten Contracts

~

Time's best friend is fear and insecurity. Its greatest disguise is free will and choice. And its greatest enemy, me.

~

I will have to break your legs, my friend. You will have to be brought down to your knees. Do you agree?

Yes.

~

I will take him away. He will be gone from your life, forever. Do you accept?

Yes.

~

You will know nothing. You will understand nothing for years, even decades.
Do you accept?

Yes.

~

Restlessness and struggle will be the order of the day, for years, even decades.
Do you accept?

Yes.

~

You will not know what is real. You will be unable to distinguish,
for a long time. Do you accept?

Yes.

~

You will believe that I forgot about you, forgot all about you. Do you accept?
Yes.

~

You will believe that I betrayed you, that I let you down. Do you accept?
Yes.

~

I will give her to you and then take her away. Do you accept?
Yes.

~

You will believe you let me down. You will believe. Do you accept?

Yes.

~

You will believe you betrayed me. You will believe. Do you accept?

Yes.

~

You will believe that your children have abandoned you. Do you accept?

Yes.

~

You will believe you abandoned your children. Do you accept?

Yes.

~

Those near to you will fail to understand you. Do you accept?

Yes.

~

Others will succeed at work, while you survive. Do you agree?

Yes.

~

She will run away with someone else. She will. Do you agree?

Yes.

~

You will run away with someone else. You will. Do you agree?

Yes.

~

The one you love will judge you. Do you agree?

Yes.

~

Love grows deeper. Or falls by the wayside.
Everything is written in your contract. But live your truth.
Live your truest truth, despite the contract.

~

A contract will fulfill itself, despite your efforts to fight it or follow it.

~

You may break the contract, after it has been fulfilled and its purpose served.

~

Contracts may extend or shorten, as I see fit.

~

Judge not your own contract, as this will cause unnecessary suffering.
Live it with a smile. Live it with dignity.

~

Always remember that every broken contract must be fulfilled at a later time.

~

Lastly, know that I seek those who seek me. None else.
Let the rest keep busy with this world.

~

The Ship That's Always Sinking

~

"What are you waiting for, my friend?" The Madman repeated. "Let nothing stop you now. Nothing."

~

I must find the truth. Myself. There is no other way. No one can guide you. No one, I thought to myself, for the first time, even though I had known it all along. Some things were such.

~

The illusion of independence is a gift to you. For you exist not as the separate entity you believe yourself to be.

~

"The only reason why two people can't stay away from each other is because of a third thing that emerges when they are together," The Strange One said to me. "It's the presence of God, from which no one can stay away."

~

There would be no one to show me the way. I knew this now.

Perhaps just The Voice. But today, I couldn't hear that, either. Nor could I feel its silence.

~

"And this is the way it shall be, from here on," The Voice said, just when I thought it had disappeared.

~

Remember that silence is greater than all the voices in the world.

~

Was this the last time I will hear it? I wondered.

It was a scary thought. Losing The Voice.

But I was ready today to let it go as well.

I was ready to let it all go.

~

Except her.
She would have to let him go.

~

The one thing you cannot let go is the very thing you will have to let go.
It is written.
In our contract.

~

These are the words you do not want to hear. The words you will never hear.

~

"I must go back. I must," I replied. The Madman continued smiling at me.

~

. . . time is running out, my love. It is. And I will be left behind for sure . . .

~

There was no struggle to reach the surface, for suddenly I found myself back on the waves, swimming easily towards the ship that I saw sailing in the distance.

~

All is well. Things are moving swiftly according to plan. One way or another.

~

Of course, it would be there, I had no doubt at all. For this was the ship that cannot sink. And this was the ship that was always sinking.

~

I swam steadily towards the ship that looked as beautiful as it ever did, swaying gently with the waters, proudly holding its mast up.

The black skies were gone, and it was like any other day. As I got closer to the ship, I could hear the shipmen's voices. Or perhaps I imagined hearing them, in anticipation. They threw the rope to me, and from the side of the ship, I climbed back to the deck, where I saw for the first time that the shipmen looked different. Perhaps I had a fresh pair of eyes now. Or perhaps I had never really noticed them. After all, the only friends I had on the ship were The Lead Shipman, The Leper, The Winemaker, and The Madman, if he could be considered a friend, that is. But they all smiled warmly at me as I climbed aboard.

"Welcome aboard, son," The Captain said, standing at his customary place on the upper deck.

Nothing could describe the happiness I felt upon seeing him. Nothing. "How did the ship survive the wave?" I asked, my eyes searching for The Lead Shipman.

"It was The Captain. He saved this ship," one of the shipmen said. I remembered him vaguely from before, but today I saw his sparkling greenish-brown eyes and his bright, wide smile for the first time.

"We survived it, my friend," The Lead Shipman said. "We are alive."

"But the wave was too big," I said to him. "You know how big it was. It would have been impossible to . . ."

"We lost The Madman," The Lead Shipman said, with his eyes down.

"They are safe, I am sure," I said. The shipmen looked puzzled.

"God bless his soul," The Lead Shipman said. "May he find whatever he was looking for . . . Or whatever was looking for him."

I looked up at The Captain with a thousand questions.

~

"Don't ever leave me. Don't let me go," she said.

Was he dreaming? he couldn't tell . . .

"It was never me, my dear," he replied. "It was always you."

~

"Sometimes I go into the small cabin on the upper deck, the one that lies empty at all times, and I stay there, drinking, reading, and smoking my cigar, for days or weeks, even months—I cannot tell," The Captain spoke slowly. Why didn't anyone look in there? I wondered. He walked towards me as I was talking to the shipmen. "Sometimes I have been told that years had passed . . . sometimes even decades or more. There were times when I came out and not a soul even recognized me. Not a soul."

I could say nothing.

"Not a soul," he repeated. "Not a soul."

We didn't know what to say.

"You must be famished," he said. "Give him something to eat, will you?" he yelled.

"How did you do it, sire? How did you save this ship?" I asked The Captain. "You must answer me."

"No miracle, son," he replied, speaking to all of us. "Just an old trick of mine which I shall teach you all soon enough."

And he walked away before I could ask any more questions.

~

"I am in debt, man. Need to pay it off," I said.

"Finances. Don't let them get you down," a friend replied. "Far heavier is the weight of loyalty . . ."

I was silent.

Was loyalty a burden or a choice? Sometimes it was hard to tell.

~

"It was The Captain who steered the ship to safety after you jumped off," The Lead Shipman said to me, handing me the broth.

"I didn't jump off," I said to him, in as calm a voice as I could manage. "It took me, the wave."

"You jumped before the wave reached us," he replied.

"That's not how it happened," I said, but I wasn't completely sure.

~

A Captain never abandons his ship. Never.

~

"Fear can do strange things to us, my friend. Strange things. So I judge you not," he said. "Who knows what I would do when faced with certain death?"

What really happened? I wondered. I knew nothing. Nothing.

"But how did the ship survive?" I asked.

"The Captain asked us all to go down to the hull and row. He wanted none on the upper deck. And before we knew it, we were floating on the sea, safe and sound. The ship needs some repair, but it was a miracle; that's all I can say. Our Captain will never let us down—he won't. I know this now for sure. More than I ever did." He smiled. "Good to have you back, my friend."

~

We rebuilt the ship that week. And we mourned not for The Madman. This was the life on the ship. And every night that week, The Captain drank like a fish.

"I wonder who will be the next to leave the ship," he said. "I wonder who will jump."

But those words didn't touch me, even though I heard them. Perhaps they were for someone else.

I was back on the ship. And this is all that mattered to me.

~

"My ship is always sinking. But it will never sink," The Captain said, quaffing another cup. "My ship travels with me. I do not travel with the ship."

I couldn't understand him.

~

The Promise That Cannot Be Broken

~

It was many years ago—or decades; I do not know—but one night, when our spirits soared and the wine surged through our blood like never before, we spoke our greatest truths to each other.

"Promise me that you will be with me forever, that you shall never leave my side," The Captain had asked me, putting his hand forward to shake mine. He was slouched in his chair that night, and I listened carefully to what he said, for I knew that every word uttered by The Captain meant something. I knew that now. And I knew that then, too.

"I promise," I said, without a moment's hesitation. And we shook hands. "But you, too, must promise me that you will take me with you, wherever you go."

~

"Don't live for each other, my friends. Live through each other," The Captain said. "Die with those who fell off the ship. Swim with those who are still afloat. And row with us, those who still live in the hope of finding the promised land. Live with the one you wait for. And live with the one who waits for you. Live through them all. Live through them all."

I sat in the corner of the ship listening. Just listening.

"And live not for me. Live not for me," he repeated. "For I am the one who will live through you."

~

I immediately felt lighter.

~

The Captain's words were much more than words to me that day. They were balm to my soul, and the truth they carried resounded in every cell of my body that day.

Hallelujah, praise the lord! I said, loudly, in my heart, and I smiled to myself.

For a part of me had truly left this ship along with The Madman, even though I did not go with him.

~

He had said to me many years ago, when I had just met Him: "I will take you where you want to go. Just hang on—that's all. Don't leave. I do whatever is required. Whatever is required to get you there."

And those words had imprinted themselves in my mind and heart so deeply, that each time I wanted to leave, I could never do it.

After all, I *had* to get there. At any cost.

~

He had walked for so many days and months—past the forest, past the river, the hills, and onto the high plains—that when he saw her, he could hardly believe his eyes. It was as if he were seeing a human being for the very first time in his life.

And she was no ordinary being. Her eyes sparkled, and her face was radiant and open, with a strength he hadn't quite seen before.

~

"The skies are bright and blue today, but do not be fooled," The Captain said. "For much happens in this world of which we know not. And much changes within, quietly, in this silence that precedes the storm. You, my faithful comrades, have not much you can lose. But this is not the end, my friends. It is the fire that appears to blow itself out before it consumes the entire forest and burns the seas. Imagine yourself lying down on a bed, motionless, unable to get up, even though your eyes are open. You know it not, but you are waiting. And you know not that you are waiting."

I barely heard what he said. For my mind was too empty of everything to understand sentences such as these.

"So be patient, and know that all is moving according to plan. I speak to those who will remember. And I remind you once again, as these are the words that you will not hear. Even if I say so myself," he spoke slowly, leaving large silences between the words. I was the only one present in his company today. The rest were busy repairing the ship, as per his orders.

~

She looked me straight in the eye, until I could meet her gaze no more.

"Why are you here?" she asked me.

"I have been traveling from the south," I said. "I have no reason."

"Everything must have a reason, should it not?" she said, her eyes twinkling.

"It must. But we don't always know them, do we?"

"Perhaps we choose not to know them," she said and continued, "I stay in that village yonder." She pointed towards a clump of trees in the distance.

"Is that so?"

"Would you like to rest for a while before you move ahead? You would enjoy a wholesome meal, I am sure," she said. "And a good night's rest."

I nodded. It was nothing short of a miracle.

"You are too kind. Truly," I said.

"Any guest is to be treated as God. We were taught this by our ancestors," she said, as her long, thick hair caught the wind. "So feel not obliged. It is our way—that is all. Follow me." And she strode ahead without a moment's delay.

~

A Game of Chess

~

My wish from decades ago had been granted. I did nothing on the ship but stare at the sea all day, take a swim now and then, and lie down in my cabin. The ship was rebuilt in a week, and it looked healthy and strong. The boy with the green eyes was turning out to be The Captain's favorite, as he was exactly what the ship needed—a boy full of life, with a twinkle in his eyes.

"This is my boy! He still dreams, he believes in me, and that is what nourishes me on this journey I have undertaken," The Captain announced loudly, while the boy smiled happily.

~

I had stopped dreaming. And the ship must have been slower for it, even if it didn't show.

I used to be like the boy, I thought to myself, as I saw his hair flying while he laughed. He reminded me of myself. But years and decades had had their way with me, and now my body was just a fraction of what it used to be. My shoulders ached, and my knees were unstable. I had blisters on my skin that itched for months at a stretch. The joints on my fingers hurt, and I could no longer carry a simple pail of water.

But all this was insignificant to me, for the last thing on my mind was my body's health. After all, the body was the vessel of the mind and heart, neither of which I could feel any more. The past was over, and hope had melted away at some point without my even realizing it.

I was on the ship. But truly, somewhere else, in a place I could not recognize.

~

The Lead Shipman did his work quietly and steadily. But one thought, like a thorn, had entered his mind and changed him. He spoke not about it. But his singing and loud yelling was replaced by a gentler tone. Perhaps he missed The Madman. Perhaps he missed me, for I was as good as absent.

"Rest a while, my friend," The Captain had said, when I reported for duty. "Do as you please on this ship. For you have missed the eye of the needle. You have escaped death for now, but it still hangs on you like a cloak. Henceforth, you are relieved of all duties on this ship, for you are no longer fit for work."

I found my lute that night, looking for a way to fill my time, but my fingers had hardened now. They refused to move.

There was no music to play.

~

BOOK XIII

~

Be grateful when you have everything. Be grateful when you have nothing.
And flowers shall bloom on the path that you tread upon.

~

You cannot long for what you have not tasted.

~

The Forgotten Son

~

It was not they who forgot me. It was not Him who forgot me. It was not she who forgot me. And it was not God who forgot me.

It was I who had forgotten myself.

It was I.

~

The story was perfect as it was.

It was just me who was missing.

~

Nothing will ever add up. Nothing.

Your peace lies within.

~

He was born in the month of September or October. The exact date of his birth was unknown. He was told it was almost a full moon that night. That is all he was told. It was a quiet affair. There was just one other person in the room. His mother clenched the piece of wood in her mouth and accepted the pain. His father was elsewhere, in another land, far away, he was told, and one day he would be back. He would certainly be back, he was told for many years after.

~

She was the local medicine woman in the village, and when she returned to her locked home after many months, she brought back the fairest child in the land, with eyes that sparkled like the brightest stars and skin that shone like gold.

"He has no mother or father. He was left in the chapel at night so I took him as my own," she had said to everyone in the village, smiling, kissing the child on his soft cheeks. But they all knew the truth. And even she knew that she was fooling no one. But some things were better like that.

That evening, when all the women of the village came to her house with pies and the tastiest sweets made by their own hands and took turns holding the baby, she felt she had a family. It was not the perfect family, but it was still family. But at night, after they'd all left and she was alone with the sleeping child, she cried for the child. For she knew that the man she'd taken as her husband, the father of her child, would not be back for a long time . . . a very long time. But one day the child would have his father. One day. She lived in the hope. But the hope was shattered when she found out seven years later that he had died in a forest fire. That's when she knew he would never, ever return.

~

My Dearest,

I know you have a wife, your own children and obligations that you must fulfill, but I now carry your child in my womb. I expect nothing from you. But remember always, if you will, that you have a family here as well. A family that you can choose to embrace whenever the time is right. I leave that to you. But I am going to have this child, and I am happy to have it and know that it is yours. Feel not sad for me, for God will look after us, and it is with His grace that I am loved by all in this village for the work I do. He has been kind to me, and so, worry not for your child who lives without his father. And worry not for me even though I miss you terribly. For in the end, it is all in the Lord's hands.

Yours.

~

Just like him, his mother was never one to speak too many words. But she told him of this letter many years later, when he turned twelve. She also told him his father would never return because he was no more. He was not shocked, for children knew most things before they were spoken. Instead, he held his mother in his hands as she sobbed. "He loved me. He did," she said to him. "As I loved him." And he believed her. She was telling the truth. He could feel it in her voice.

~

When he was seventeen, and old enough to chart the course of his own life, he told his mother one night, sitting next to her on the bed, "I wish to go to the village where my father once lived."

"But he is no more," she replied. "You know that. I lie not to you."

"I know, mother. I still wish to go."

"But why, son?" she asked him. "There is nothing there for you."

"Even so. I must go." he said gently, holding her hand. Why he said this he did not fully understand. But it was clear to him. He had no choice in the matter.

"I will be back soon, mother," he said to her. "I go with your blessings."

"God bless you, my child." She smiled. "I wish to see you happy—that is all."

"I know, mother," he said, getting up to his room to take his belongings. "I will write you from there."

~

He had found a place to live, an old dilapidated room that he could barely afford, and found, by some stroke of luck, a job as the local blacksmith's apprentice. He spent the days surrounded by the scalding heat of melting iron that turned his hands and face red and brown. And his soft, golden hair was black with grime and soot.

The nights were lonely, but he had made a few friends at the local tavern where he would slowly sip on a cup of cheap ale, for that is all he could afford. Occasionally, the old man who served him would fill his empty cup without asking for a single coin. His nature was such. People came forward to help him, wanting nothing in return. "What is it you seek here, lad?" the old man had asked him once. "This village has not much to offer."

"Perhaps you do not see the value of your own kindness and that of the others in this village, then," he replied.

"A toast to the young stranger who is certainly wiser than his years. Be not deceived by his boyish face, burnt as it may be!" the old man said out loud for all to hear that night. The others clapped and cheered, and came around to talk to him. And in an instant, he felt at home. But he hadn't truly answered the old man's question. Some things should not be rushed, he thought to himself, for he was in no haste to find his father's family.

~

Leave yourself behind. Walk free from all that shackles you. Lead not your life. It was never yours, anyway. It was mine. It was mine.

~

"There's nothing here for me," I said. "I want to leave."

"But the gift is coming—can't you see it? Unless there's something the world has to offer that you want . . . In which case, you should go."

"There's nothing out there, either," I said. "That's the problem."

~

You cannot long for what you have already eaten.

~

And you cannot long for that which you have never tasted.

~

This book you read.
Have you heard a single word of it?
Have you taken in a single line?

~

It was late in the evening when I stood at the back of the ship, with my hands on the side of *the deck. I could see the sunset and hear the sounds of the water. But inside me was a hole, an emptiness that disconnected me from all of it. Nothing made a difference anymore. Neither the passing storm, nor the bright yellow sun or the blue skies. Truly, I saw nothing and felt nothing, for my senses were no longer connected to my heart and mind. And I could feel, since I had returned to the ship, that something wasn't right. The past was clear. It was my present that was blurry.*
Was this happening to me? Or was I doing this to myself? I could not tell.

~

A man can change his life in a single moment. But for that he must let go of what he holds on to the most. Or face what he fears the most.
God neither waits for him nor obstructs him in this endeavor. It is the way of life.

~

As I walked behind her, I remembered him. He had come looking for me, even though he didn't know it. And I was destined to find him, even though I didn't know it. It was the day when the rain gods were angry and water poured down in sheets, flooding the village. I was fifteen years old when I walked into the tavern for the very first time that night. After four full cups of ale, I had lost all control.

He saw me struggling to walk straight and put his arm around my shoulder. "Let's get you home, boy," he said. "Tell me where you live."

"Thank you, friend. You are truly a kind soul," I had said to him as he knocked on my door while holding me up straight.

My mother answered the door.

"He's had a cup too many," he said to her.

She should have been upset with her son. But she felt none of that. There was something about this young man. He rarely looked up but even so, she could simply not take her eyes off him.

"He will sleep it off," she said. "And who are you, young man? Come in and sit down for a bit."

~

The things we do that have no reasons behind them are perhaps the truest guides of our lives, I thought to myself.

~

I could feel myself leaning towards the blue waters down below, inside which time had stood still and answers came before questions. But that, too, was a distant memory. The sense of being needed on this ship, much less being the next Captain of this ship, had faded away fast. For The Captain's disappearance was a lie. We would be reaching no promised land, even if it did exist.

What was I alive for? What was the wish and dream in my heart that fueled this ship?

I could feel nothing. The only thing left inside me was the promise I had made to The Captain—the promise that could not be broken. The promise I had made, truth be told, to myself and told myself a thousand times I would never break.

It was this that had slowly become a wish in my heart . . . a wish that had gone deeper inside me than love itself.

~

In time, we became the best of friends, for we shared much in common—our love for music, for adventure, and our dreams for the future. We would sit by the lake and talk of all that we wanted to do, all that life had in store for us, and what this world was truly made of. We would carry a small piece of bread with dried fruit to eat and climb the hills a few miles away from the village. We would sit on top of the hill, sweaty and tired, and look into the distance at the setting sun and the beautiful purple-pink skies. I would carry with me sheets of paper and make little flying triangles that slowly made their way down to the plains. Some would catch the wind and fly higher than where we stood, and we would smile, as a part of us flew just as high as the little pieces of folded paper.

"Let's be on our way now. We must reach the bottom of the hill before it gets dark," he would say as the light began to disappear. He was always thinking about everything.

"One more," I would say, quickly pulling out a sheet and folding it. I wanted to see it fly over the hills just once more, before we scratched our legs against the thorny bushes as we rushed down the hill.

"Quickly then," he would say impatiently, as he folded his hands and waited a few moments before he decided not to wait anymore for me. For he knew it would be dark in no time and that coming down the hill would take twice the time as it normally would. "I'm leaving now," he would say, leaving me to decide for myself what I wanted to do.

~

The Captain had said to me a long time ago, "I live for you all. It is you all that keep me alive, for I have no other reason to be here. I have already reached my shore, a long time ago." I remembered his words today, as I felt the wind blowing through my hair.

The young boy with green eyes came up and stood next to me. "It's a beautiful adventure, isn't it? I love the smell of this ship, and every moment with The Captain is a surprise." He had a habit of finding me in my quiet moments and talking to me. "There is so much to learn from you all. So much. Especially those like you, who have been here for so long."

"You have learned from me?" I said, surprised.

"Of course, sire. I have watched you and learned many things from you. Your cheerful smile. Your good humor. Your honesty. But most of all, your faith in The Captain."

"I have lost faith in myself and in everything, my friend. There is nothing more anyone can learn from me. Death hangs like a cloak on me, and you and I both know my time on this ship is soon coming to an end."

"Do you not enjoy this life anymore?" he continued. "You used to. Not long ago. You used to."

"I am tired, my friend. Very tired," I said. "There's nothing The Captain says that ignites my heart anymore. Nothing."

"I will miss you, sire. Very much," he said. I could see tears welling up in his eyes. "You and The Captain are all I have. I cannot imagine this ship without you. I cannot."

I never knew till today of what was in the boy's heart. And I had no words to say to him. I knew exactly what he was feeling. Exactly. For what he said to me was what I had said many times to The Captain in my heart, though never to him in person. I had cried many a night in despair when The Captain appeared to have disappeared from the ship. It was only then that I had truly missed his laughter, his temper, his arrogance, and his good humor. Most of all, I missed the conversations we had at night, after many a cup of wine. But I was no longer part of those conversations, nor did I wish to be. For he said the same thing over and over again. The same thing. Over and over.

~

Let go of yourself. Live for others, and you shall find your eternal self.
This is what The Voice said.
But was it telling me the truth? I didn't know what to believe.

~

The Village Palm Reader

~

When I slept that night, it was as if the ship had come to a complete halt. I could feel no swaying at all. Not even the slightest bit. And the ship was certainly not moving forward. I knew, at all times, like any other shipman, how fast the ship was moving. Even in my sleep.

Tonight, I could not hear the waters or the sound of the shipmen in the distance. I lay in my bunk like it was the bed of a King, wide and soft, in a sleep so restful that the tiredness of lifetimes seemed to melt away. Had we reached land? I wondered as I awoke to the gentle light of the sun before it rose. But this was hope speaking, I knew, even before I walked out onto the upper deck to see the ship sailing silently towards the southwest.

~

"Only those who can watch these magnificent floods wipe away our crops and destroy the land that we have tilled with our very own hands—only they can play this game of loss and gain tomorrow. This world is already too full of trad-ers. Remember . . . those fearful of loss cannot play with the elements." The King had spoken that day. But we heard it not. For we were all in tears watching the tender saplings floating like corpses on the waters that lapped at our feet.

~

The Captain was awake early that morning. And even though just a few of us were present on the upper deck as the sun rose, he strode in and spoke loud enough for us to hear. "Stay with me, friends, as I sink this ship or make it fly. Play this game of life and death. Play without fear, with-out the promise of a dream, and with nothing to profit. For it is fear, hope, and profit that take you away from your destination."

I listened to every word as if they were for me and me alone.

"The dream ends not, sometimes, when you lose all hope, but when it comes true beyond your wildest imagination." The Captain's words were clear and crisp today.

~

As she strode ahead of me, I looked at the pastures on either side. They were full of life and innocence. The leaves of grass grew thick and sprung out from the earth with the gentle strength of life wanting to live itself. Not a soul looked after the land here, but the grass coated the hills so perfectly, it was as if God himself had tilled and seeded the land. I could see the perfection today, even though I had grown up on lands that looked no different than this.

"Where is your family?" she asked, as we walked.

"In the south. My mother and my two sisters," he replied.

"And your father?"

"He died in a forest fire, many years ago, when I was a child."

"I'm sorry to hear that," she said, calmly.

"Perhaps it is all destined," I said. "Who knows where life would have taken me, had he been alive? I may have been a carpenter."

"I'm sure you would have made a good one," she said, taking my hand in hers. "Your fingers are skilled, but your skin is delicate. And your nature, brooding. Too much philosophy can do that to you."

"How can you tell? Do you read palms?" I asked.

"Yes, I am the village palm reader." She smiled. "But from your hands I see you believe not in the mystic sciences. You place your faith in your intelligence."

"You may be right," I said, thinking about what she just said. "But I have no interest in philosophy. You are certainly wrong about that."

"I do not know if I am right or wrong. That is not for me to say. I speak only what the hands speak." She said. "Perhaps, you know not what you are. For all travelers who travel without a purpose must be philosophical. They seek something although they know not what they seek."

"Some may be running away from something," I replied.

"Isn't it quite the same?" She smiled.

~

The Tree of Life

~

It was a small village, not unlike the one I came from. But here I could hear the laughter of children and the chattering of old men and women all around. Where I came from, it was quiet, almost always.

"You may stay here for as long as you wish," she said, offering me a bowl of chicken broth and sprinkling freshly plucked parsley over it. "But if you wish to make yourself useful, you could help my father. He is the village butcher."

"Thank you. I know not why I deserve this kindness," I said.

"What you deserve is not my concern," she replied, in the same manner that was neither warm nor cold. "You are tired, and you need much rest before you can move on ahead. You will need a strong body and great faith, both of which you lack."

"Is this written in my hands?" I asked. "What else can you tell me?"

"I have told you everything your hands have said to me." She looked at me with a straight gaze.

"I have no strength and no faith," I said. "I am of no use to anyone."

"That is not for you to determine." She smiled. "Those who are of no use can be used by forces unknown to me and you."

I kept silent.

"Eat this fresh bread, and sleep now. Your bed is made," she said, pointing to the door on the other side of the house as she walked away.

~

Miracles do happen, I thought to myself, as I lay on a bed this comfortable after so long.

Was God watching over me? I wondered.

~

"New journeys will be made. New wings will be grown. New gardens will be found, new seeds will be sown, and forgotten smiles remembered," The King had said one evening as we drank the broth we drank every day and ate the bread we ate every day. But we knew not what he spoke about. This morning, as I woke up in a place that suddenly felt like home, I remembered his words. The birds chirped, and the sun's morning rays turned the tender green leaves on the tree outside my window into thousands of little emeralds that dangled from above.

The smell of the earth reminded me that all of this was a gift. How easy it was to forget that nothing was owed to you. How easy it was to forget that it was all His creation.

"Would you like some tea?" the palm reader said, standing at my door. She was beautiful in every sense. But I could not love her or desire her. She wanted nothing from me, I knew. There was nothing in me she disliked. And nothing in me that she found special. And this made love, as I knew it, impossible.

"Yes. That would be perfect," I replied, embarrassed by my own thoughts for a moment. Could she read my mind, too? I wondered.

"After you bathe and put on some fresh clothes, you can go to our shop. My father will be waiting for you."

"Yes. Certainly," I said. I had always avoided The Butcher's shop in our village. The sight of blood nauseated me. But the choice was not mine to make this time. I could not refuse her.

~

I got the call that evening. From Him.

"There's an assignment in Baku. In Azerbaijan. It's for a month. Do you want to go?"

"Yes." There was no hesitation. Neither in my words nor in my heart.

~

And a part of me knew I wasn't coming back. Not for a long time.

~

September 25, 2013

BOOK XIV

~

The Planter of Seeds

~

The story you write is your incomplete life expressing itself. For what you have truly lived, need never be spoken or written about.
It is complete. Finished.

~

Those who let you down also set you free.

~

When you have run out of places to go to is when you will have to live with yourself.

~

"We treat every animal with care," he said, showing me around the shop. "Never disregard the life that has to give itself up in order for you to live."

The Palm Reader's father was a a man of small stature, though much stronger than he looked. The veins under the skin of his wiry arms were clearly visible as he picked up things and put them in their rightful place. And the shop was surprisingly clean, considering that the animals were regularly butchered. In the front of the shop, the meat hung on iron hooks.

"I will explain your work to you later on." He smiled, sitting on a chair. "Let us talk for a while."

"Of course, sir," I said.

"Where do you come from, lad? And what is your religious denomination?

"From the south. I was born to a Christian family," I replied. "But truly, I know not if God exists."

He said nothing.

"If He does, then certainly, I cannot understand the reason for why things are the way they are. Or why they happen the way they happen . . ."

"Are you married?"

I was quiet for a moment. He waited for an answer.

"I have no wife," I replied. But this was not a conversation I wanted to have. "What denomination do you follow here, in this village, if I may ask?"

"I follow nothing," he said. "But you could call me a student of the Kabbalah."

"What is that, if I may ask? And what does it say about God? And heaven or hell."

"The Kabbalah is as ancient as life itself. It is a way of receiving, a way to an understanding of everything. All is one, and whatever exists in this universe, heaven or hell, is all part of the divine creation," he said, slowly. "But these words mean nothing unless you know this for yourself."

"Can one not study it?"

"Study is but a preparation for greater knowledge, the kind of which is found not in books, but within your own soul."

"You are a true scholar, then," I said.

"I have read but a book or two. That hardly makes me a scholar." He smiled again. "They say that understanding even one simple line of a holy book is all one needs. It has to be felt deep within yourself, they say. Like love, perhaps."

I was silent. The very mention of that word instantly created an empty, hollow sensation in my heart.

"I fear I cannot feel love again," I said. "But I wish to learn whatever I can from you. It would be my honor."

He smiled. I smiled back.

"If that smile was real, then love is already finding its way inside your heart. For what is love but laughter and contentment . . . It includes all. This emptiness of yours as well."

I said nothing, but my soul felt at peace. And today, despite all the blood and flesh that was around me, I felt no nausea.

None at all.

~

"There are four ways in which something may be understood. These are the four doors of perception. First is the simple meaning. This is the most easy and direct," he said, while we drank hot tea in the late afternoon. "But what is simple to understand is rarely understood by the heart, other than by those who are truly simple."

"How so?"

"Take what I said earlier. That all is one." He closed his eyes for a moment. "Easy to understand by most, but not truly understood."

I smiled.

"The second is indirect. Such as a simple image or situation that allows great truths to penetrate your heart."

"Can you explain?"

"Hmm." He thought for a moment. "Imagine an old ship that sails endlessly on the wide seas, and imagine all those who live on board and wait to reach land without knowing if or when they will ever reach."

I could see it immediately.

"And the ship never quite reaches." He smiled. "It's the story of our life, isn't it?"

"Yes," I replied. "It most certainly is."

~

Everything you have ever lived has its seeds from before. For no tree exists which did not sprout from a seed so small and yet so large that it contains within it the destiny of every leaf that grows upon it.

~

When there is no one to talk to, God becomes your best friend.

~

When I awoke that day, I felt young again. It was as if the same body now contained within it a younger self. I went and lay down on the upper deck, enjoying the cool breeze and the sound of the ocean that felt new to me all over again. And before I knew it, the sun was setting, and pink clouds were scattered across the purple skies. Time is truly the most mysterious thing God has ever created, I thought. I imagined a time when all was still, and not a thing or a soul moved. What difference would a thousand years make to a barren land with no life, no wind, no fire and no water? Absolutely nothing.

I climbed down from the upper deck and saw on my way the boy with the green eyes working hard at the sail. He looked tired, and his face, usually bright and fresh, was today sullen and grim.

"What is it, lad?" I walked over to him and placed my hand on his shoulder.

"How long can this ship sail anyway? And how long must we struggle to keep it afloat? I have faith in The Captain—I do. But life has become so dreary, I would rather this ship sink and take us all down with it. I wish for nothing any more. Nothing." He was almost in tears now.

"You are much too young to speak like this, lad," I said. "Much too young."

"Perhaps because you do, sire?" he said impertinently.

I struggled for an answer.

"Perhaps this is what our Captain wants—to break our spirits until we can live no more," he said, and the others looked at me for an answer.

"No, my friend, no!" I said. "What did you all know of friendship, loyalty, or faith, before you set yourself upon this ship? What did you know of life or death?"

They were all quiet.

"Nothing. You all know nothing," I said. "This land that you hunger for is where you have come from. And it is a prison much worse than what you believe this to be."

They listened carefully.

"The ship shall sail on, my friends." I said. And for the first time in my life, it was exactly what I wanted. The ship had to sail. And it most certainly would, until my breath carried me on this earth.

And they all cheered and smiled with the fullness of their hearts.

"For if this ship sinks, then so shall all your ships, my friends. So shall all your dreams, and so shall all your friends who have come to be your family now," I continued. "Remember that, on this ship, each one of you is the Captain of his own ship. And that ship is your unfolding destiny. It remains unseen until you dig deep within your soul and discover who you are."

"So drink your wine if you are tired, my green-eyed friend, and the morning will find you different one day, as I find myself today," I said, looking at the boy. "Everything passes. So let us bring cheer in our hearts and smile into the winds as we sail forth. And if we are lucky enough, a beautiful mermaid, which even I have never laid my eyes upon, may chance upon us as she swims deep in the ocean down below."

And with that thought, the green-eyed boy slept, and that single thought turned into a thousand dreams in his heart.

And the ship didn't just sail swiftly that night. The winds blew like never before, almost lifting the ship as it skimmed over the waves.

~

The Burden of Guilt

~

"Be thankful, my friends, when people need you not, when you are truly forgotten," I said to them the next day in the lower deck, holding my cup of wine. I had drunk more than six cups that day. "Remember that, to be invisibly in each other's hearts is a place akin to heaven itself. So rejoice, my friends, and let us all disappear, so that none remain, and only the Lord's light shines bright from within."

The boy with the green eyes smiled at me, pouring another serving of wine into my empty cup.

"Tell us more," he said to me. But my mind was blank, for what I spoke echoed in my ears as it did in his.

"Don't make me think, lad. I cannot speak when I think," I said and walked away towards my cabin.

~

I say unto you: Drop this burden, and then lift what you will.
Lift what you will.

~

"Never forget The Captain. Never," I said to them today. "Just like your breath that breathes you."

They listened to him, stopping themselves from whatever they were doing that morning.

"Till the day you know it, the truth needs to be repeated, again and again, till it flows as the blood does through your veins. Till then."

~

"The time has come for you to meet the father," The Captain said in my dreams as I woke up that cool morning. "For he is your father, as he is mine. And he creates you in his image as he created me in his. And when all around you has turned into dust, He will be there, all around you, and inside you, just like the water is to the fish that live in it. This was our contract, and I have kept my promise, as did you. As did you."

~

"It is usually the loss of love that brings one to mysticism, son," he said. "But study is just preparation for passing through the trials and tribulations of life. And this, too, is Torah. For Torah is not just the study of scriptures, but a state of learning."

"I would like to learn more, sir, if I may," I said, "For I have lost love and all things good that come along with it."

"History can be learned. Crafts and mathematics can be learned," he replied. "But to know life itself, the time must be right."

"If anyone's time has come, it would be mine, sir," I replied.

"Is that for you to determine?" His words were sharp. "Pride and self-judgment have no place here, son. Either you will teach me, or I will teach you. There is no other way."

166

"Please, sir, forgive me my error." I sat up. "It is I who have come here to learn from you."

"But I will learn a thing or two from you, too, my friend." He smiled, and his eyes twinkled. "For I am sure your travels have taken you to places that I have never laid my eyes upon."

"Travels are of no use, when the heart is hollow and empty, sir," I said.

"It appears you may be ready to learn after all," he said.

"I fear this pain I carry may never leave me," I said.

"But it is not pain that one carries," he said. "It is the burden of guilt and anger with the self that can haunt a man past his own lifetime."

I didn't understand that immediately. But I knew truth when it was spoken. Somehow, I did.

~

What is this burden I am carrying? I asked myself, as I lay in bed that night. For it weighed heavily on me, even though I knew of no other way to live. But years of carrying this burden was also breaking my back.

~

I thought to myself as well . . . What was in me that held me from living?

Love and loyalty . . . were they a curse . . .

Or were they the very path to my freedom? This was my unanswered question.

~

What is hidden in this book remains hidden, my friend.
Even from you, even from you.
Until you find it.
Until you find it for yourself.

~

"The third is by way of investigation," he said. We had finished our work for the day. By now I had grown accustomed to the continuous smell of flesh and blood that surrounded me. As we washed our hands, he continued, "It requires effort . . . the desire to know the truth. And to seek it with introspection and dedication."

I was listening.

"Few people are capable of this. It is not for the common man."

"But those who are ready . . . Surely they will be able to grasp the truth."

"To think correctly that all is one is different from knowing that all is one. And only by the grace of God can one truly live it."

"Do you live, good sir, as if all is one? Do you know this each and every moment?" I asked.

"By God's grace, I live in silence." He smiled gently, as the water washed away the blood from his hands. "My work. It forces me to remember."

"Can you tell me what my work is?" I asked. "For I must seek what will help me remember as well."

"What is meant to, finds us. We need not seek it," he replied.

I kept silent.

"I was looking for the magical forest not long ago . . ." I said, thinking about what he said. "But I found it not. Your daughter found me, and here I stand, learning about life from you. Was it you who sought me?"

"Knowledge was seeking you, son. Not I. Remember that only when a lesson is fully learned can you begin to understand what the lesson truly was," he said very slowly. "Is it possible to simultaneously stand on the ground and get a bird's-eye view of the terrain?"

"You mean I can never understand why I am here until I leave from here," I ventured. "Am I correct in saying this?"

"Yes," he said. "Unless you run away before your time is up."

"And how would I know my time is up?" I asked.

"Water boils at a certain point. Not a moment earlier. Not a moment earlier," he said. *"Now let's make our way home before it gets too dark."*

~

The Secret That Cannot Be Told

~

They were strange days, these days on the ship. It was as if the hopes and desires of every shipman on the ship were buried so deep within their own hearts that none of it was visible. The Lead Shipman had grown quiet, although he still ensured the ship moved swiftly ahead. There was rarely the customary merriment every night. The Captain rarely spoke, and, although he was present on the ship, I could hardly feel him. Our bodies felt disconnected from our selves. It was indeed a strange time.

~

"I think I got it. The truth of my life."

"Well, what is it?"

"I think I'm delusional. I have delusions of grandeur, amongst others. I live a lie. And I also believe that I alone can cure myself of it. What if there is something wrong with me? What if I am a little bit insane?"

"But you know this. So where's the insanity?" she said.

I had heard something like this before. In my own book.

~

But something was deeply wrong, not just with myself, but with the whole world. The greed, the violence, the destruction . . . Was it even possible to be sane in this world? If I was not separate from it, then there was no way to find my own private heaven, no matter how much I tried. I was a part of the whole, and, therefore, escape was impossible.

But life was much bigger than this world and our petty wars. For the universe was as silent as the space between the stars. There were light years of silence. And everything we struggled with was insignificant.

~

"The fourth is not a way or a door. For it is hidden. It lies as a secret that unlocks itself when the time of realization has come. It is caused and yet uncaused. It requires dedication of the highest order, but only grace causes it to reveal itself," he said, as we ate dinner that night. "Nothing more can be said about it. But they say the great ones could orchestrate a series of events that would inevitably, eventually lead to its discovery."

"Who are these great ones? And how can we find them?" I had many questions.

"Who they are, you will know once you know yourself," he replied. "And it is they who find you. Not you."

"Have you been found?"

"That is how I became a butcher, son."

"Would you take me as your student, good sir?"

"Just keep learning, son. Keep learning." He smiled. "You have been my student since you set foot in this village."

~

I went to The Captain's cabin that night for the second time since I'd boarded this ship. There were questions I had. And answers I wanted. And they could not wait. Not for a moment. I sat at the lower deck, drinking as much wine as I could, for I knew I would need all the help I could get to muster up the courage to knock on The Captain's door uninvited.

"What do you want?" he said, as he opened the door, a minute after I knocked on it. A minute that felt much longer.

"I want the truth," I said. "And . . ."

"Go to sleep," he said. "Nothing I say is of any consequence."

And he shut the door before I could say any more.

~

The Taste of Freedom

~

"Know nothing, and want nothing," he said. "Breathe deep. Breathe deep. You are as free as you want to be."

The words entered like an arrow, piercing the very depths of my soul and then exploding into a million pieces.

~

Who said these words, I did not know. Was it The Captain, The Voice, The King, or The Butcher?

I did not know.

Or perhaps this time I didn't care. I didn't want to put words into someone's mouth just because I *had* to.

For it could have been any of them.

Any of them.

Including myself.

~

Who knew . . .

~

"The passage for all knowledge is Da'at. It is the abyss. The doorway to the eternal." He spoke slowly as we sipped hot tea that cold night. "One day you will pass through this tunnel. The tunnel where nothing can be seen and none can hold your hand. You will leave your loved ones behind. And all that you have learned and hold close to you."

Have I been through such a passage? I wondered.

"They say not only that you do not recognize a thing in the tunnel but that you do not recognize yourself, either."

"Where does it lead?" I asked.

"To Keter, the source of all. The beginning. The destination."

~

My name is not God, for I am everything and the source of everything, both.
Only that which begins and ends can have a name.

~

A Meeting with God

~

"What can you tell me about Keter?" I asked as we walked to the shop the next morning.

"It is the crown of the tree of life."

I listened.

"But it is Da'at, the abyss, that man runs away from," he said. "Even death is preferable to Da'at, they say. But death is just the shadow. Real dissolution requires patience. And much anguish."

"Are we doomed to suffer in this life?" I asked. "When will it end?"

"It ends when it ends." He walked briskly, and it was hard to keep up with him. "Blame none, for it is your own. Fear none, for no one can hurt you unless you carry a wound within yourself."

"What about physical pain?" I asked.

"I speak to you now," he said. "Ask questions that pertain to you and you only, for we do not indulge in discussions. It is not the way."

~

Follow your heart, and speak your truth.
Stop living in fear of being misunderstood.

~

Being misunderstood by the ones you love and living
with that is a great discipline.

~

Language must bend for the sake of the truth, for it is but a pathway.
Never mistake the spoken and the written word for the truth itself.

~

"Ein Sof, the great nothingness, is the true nature of God."

"What does it mean?"

"That without a boundary." He paused for a moment. "For it is that which the mind can never conceive."

"Then how are we to know of it, to understand it?"

"In silence and in prayer."

~

"How does one become silent?"

"When you find everything you desire all around you."

"I desire nothing. Just peace in my soul."

"If you desired nothing, there would already be peace," he replied. "You have lost hope, my son. And losing hope is akin to losing faith in life and God himself."

"Circumstances have led me to this state, good sir."

"Yes, it was His will. But fear not, for this is not the end for you. There is more. Much more."

I felt the spark of hope entering my heart. Like a warm fire on the coldest day of winter.

~

A broken cup cannot be fixed. Set your eyes on a new horizon
and move ahead, my son. Have faith in yourself, and waver not.

And look not backwards. Look not backwards.
For what lies behind you cannot be visited ever again.

~

In the Land of Eternal Fire

~

"How do I pray when I know not whether God exists?"

"You mistake prayer for an activity, son," he replied. "There are four kinds of prayer, of which the fourth is truly considered a prayer."

I listened.

"When we ask for something that will make us happy or give us peace . . . it is of the first kind. When we ask to be guided, to become better human beings . . . it is the second kind. When we are grateful and say thanks to the Lord for everything we have been given . . . it is the third kind." He paused for a moment. "The fourth is neither an asking nor a giving of thanks. When we sit down with our eyes closed, unable to speak or think, humbled by our very existence, feeling no separation from everything that surrounds us, that is prayer."

"But you have not answered my question, good sir."

"Have I not? To be humbled by existence itself requires no God," he replied. "But for that to happen, the sadness that hangs on you like a shadow must disappear. For it is your pain and grief that will visit you when you close your eyes."

I listened carefully.

"You do not believe in God anymore because you feel betrayed by Him," he said. "And that is because you believed in Him."

I was silent.

"God is beyond belief, son. To find Him, you must disappear." He knew I didn't understand that. "The mind is incapable. It cannot know of what I speak. It cannot."

~

The light exists inside you. For when the time is right,
you will see the cosmos within.

~

The greatest secret is hidden within you. Turn your eyes within,
and the truth shall be revealed to you.

~

Yanar Dag—The Fire Mountain

~

There are places on earth where fires never stop burning from the gasses contained within the earth. Pilgrims would walk thousands of miles to visit these holy places.

It must have been close to zero degrees. Today, as I sat next to the fire, I could feel the blazing heat on my face as I watched the flames leaping upwards and sideways like a living being. I wondered how long it had been burning . . . and how long it would go on.

~

The Laws of Nature

~

It is what you know to be true that keeps you from the truth.

~

What Never Happened

~

We know more than we think we do. We know it all.
We have planned it all. Perfectly.

~

Some marriages are made in heaven. Some marriages are made on earth.
And some are made in a place that you know not yet.

~

The Life of a Shipman

~

That night, we sat together after what felt like many years. Just The Lead
Shipman and I, having a cup of wine and talking about life on the ship, about

how we had forgotten where we were headed, forgotten why we boarded this ship in the first place.

"I know of no other life," The Lead Shipman said to me. "This is my only home, if I can call it that. I cannot leave this ship, for I have nowhere to go. Nowhere."

"Sometimes, I would rather be at the bottom of the sea than on this ship," I replied.

And the conversation would end there. For what else was there left to speak? We both could feel each other's tiredness as we sipped quietly on our wine, until our heads were heavy and light, all together. After so many years, spirits no longer had the same effect they used to.

"Let's sit on the upper deck. It's been a long time since we lay down and looked at the stars," I said.

"Why not?" he said. And we went up to the same spot where we used to lie down, watch the stars, and talk about how this ship could go faster, about what land would feel like, and our time with The Captain.

This time we lay quietly, staring at the clear skies.

~

The Shooting Star

~

It came in from the east and traced the black night like a comet. And in its wake followed another two or three more.

"Make a wish," I said.

"There's nothing to wish for," he replied.

"I wish for us to laugh and be happy," I said.

He smiled. "Yes. That's a wish worth wishing."

~

Only this moment exists. Only this moment ever existed.

~

BOOK XV

~

The Day Everything Ended

~

There comes a time when you have to be honest with yourself. When you stop wondering about the story and just face yourself, your life, as it is.

~

The Real and the Unreal

~

There was no voice. They were just ideas and thoughts from my imagination.

~

This was neither The Voice of God nor messages from a distant galaxy.

~

It was just myself trying to make sense of the journey I was on.

~

"Stay silent now, my son," he said. "Conversations can give you no answers. The best ones end in silence."
I nodded.

~

Devote your life in search of the truth. Stake everything.
Only then shall you find the eternal.

~

Dreams of a Lute Player

~

I had dreamt of a balloon high in the skies, bright and colorful, in which I would travel the whole world.

~

I had dreamt of creating music like a symphony, letting the notes fall together like rivers and streams that inevitably found their way into the sea.

~

I had dreamt of waters in which I would swim endlessly without tiring, my body lithe and strong against the currents.

~

I had dreamt of gatherings with dance and laughter in the air, celebrating friendship, love, and camaraderie.

~

I had dreamt of gifting people whatever their heart wished for, things they could never have dreamt of.

~

I had dreamt of a world where children could play and learn without fear, and be left alone to discover life on their own.

~

I had dreamt of a world where anyone could talk to anyone, where everyone was a friend, even if you had never seen them before.

~

I had dreamt of animals, playing and frolicking in the sun.

~

I had dreamt of taking away another's pain, so that a smile would return to their face.

~

I had dreamt of meeting a man who lived on another plane of existence, someone I could truly learn from.

~

And, I had dreamt of her.

~

"If we understand the tree of life, then we understand ourselves," he said. "And that is the most precious thing in the world."

"May I ask you a question?"

"Yes."

"What do I need to understand?"

"Just find out the purpose of your existence," he replied. "Everything else will fall into place."

~

"My purpose is constantly changing, I believe I have no way of knowing it," I said. "I fear I cannot even think on such matters."

"No one said it would be easy, son," he replied. "Close your eyes, and ask yourself what you truly seek. Right now."

"I seek to be free from suffering," I said.

"Then that is what you shall have," he said, without a moment of hesitation.

I looked at his face for an expression. It was as if within those words were contained a farewell . . . a goodbye that was unsaid but loud enough for my heart to hear. And when I awoke the next morning, not a soul greeted me. Even The Palm Reader, who usually came to my room with my morning cup of tea, simply left the pot outside my door when I opened it.

~

When I said to him, the next morning, that I should be leaving, he was quiet for a moment.

"Leave right away, then," he said, firmly.

"Are you angry with me, sir?" I asked.

"Why would I be angry?" he replied. "I believe not in wasting time. That is all. Once a decision is made, it is best to act swiftly."

"And who will help you now at the shop?"

"This shop has been here before you and me were born, son," he said.

"Is my time here over?" I asked, revealing what was really on my mind.

"Did I ask you to leave?"

"I felt it in your words yesterday," I replied. "And your daughter seemed to indicate it as well."

"Perhaps a certain chapter is over, and another begins, right here," he replied. "You are hasty in your interpretations."

"I am sorry I misunderstood," I said.

"Trust not your senses so easily," he said. "Take your time before you reach conclusions."

I nodded. This time I knew there was no running away. I would stay until I was told to leave.

Until I was told.

~

"*To make a man meditate or pray, and never let him come to know of it, for months or years . . . That, my son, is the art of the great ones,*" The Butcher said, *as we sipped tea that evening.*

I went to my room that night and repeated his words to myself. I knew they were important. But when I awoke the next morning, I could remember nothing. It would come to me again, I hoped. It would.

~

What Never Goes Away

~

There are, buried within, deep-seated fears from so long ago . . . I believe they may never go away.

They will. They will.

~

There are things we hold on to that we can never let go of.

We will. We will.

~

The Unpalatable Truth

~

How else could you be led to the truth other than through the greatest illusion?

~

"As you reach the abyss, your mind will drive you insane," The Butcher said, as he scraped the fat off the freshly cut flesh. "Nothing will make sense. You will hang on to anything you can, as if your very life depends on it. Remember this."

~

I remembered it today.

~

"How else do I keep a man alive on this godforsaken ship, my friend?" The Captain said in my dreams. "I create hope. I pull it out from the depths of your heart."

~

What was He saying to me?

~

"Till you find the real coin, the false one will suffice," he said. "And to dream of the real coin is an impossibility."

"There is no promised land, is there?" I asked.

"Not the kind you are looking for," he replied, smiling.

~

And at that moment, it felt as if the ground beneath us shook. The whole ship shook like we were in the very heart of an earthquake.

"Listen, my trusted friends," The Captain said out loud for all to hear. "The time has come to leave the seas."

We all gathered at the deck, nervous but also happy.

"I may be a rogue or a madman, but a liar I am not," he said loud and clear.

I could feel my heart beating fast.

"You have waited long enough, long enough. And you stood by my side, willingly or unwillingly. That was enough."

We listened carefully, like never before.

"Worry not for those who left the ship, for it is I who let them go," he said. "They, too, like you, move towards the promised land."

I felt happy to hear those words, as did The Lead Shipman.

"Now we move forward. Above these seas and unrelenting waves," he said. "Remember, my friends, this is no ordinary ship."

And as the words were spoken, an enormous white mast, shaped like a balloon, blew up from the centre of the ship and opened up into the blue skies above. The shipmen ran towards the raging fire at the center that sent the hot air below into the circular mast that swelled and grew like a storm gathering strength. How did it work? They wondered. I looked at the boy with the green eyes and saw him laughing as he spoke to his fellow shipmen. A part of my heart exploded like the mast that was now gigantic in size. And a part of me watched it all unfolding as if I was hardly present on the ship.

"How beautiful the sea looks from above," The Captain said, as we gently lifted off the waters and rose towards the skies. The waves that we battled day and night now looked like tiny white shells, glistening on the vast blue sea.

It was for the very first time in our lives that we saw the world from above. And the feeling was indescribable.

Time stood still. We were speechless. Not a soul could utter a word. We watched silently the earth grow smaller beneath us as we flew higher and higher. The beauty and magic were overwhelming. And the ship moved swifter than ever before.

The Captain's Secret

~

"There are many things you do not know, my friends," he said, as the shipmen cheered on. "I have many a trick up my sleeve. Many a trick."

But while all the shipmen cheered and sang, I walked to the side of the ship and stood by the railings, looking down at the shimmering waters.

What was there for me on land? I wondered. It had nothing to offer me anymore. Nothing.

The loss of memory was a gift to those who could not remember. But for me, it was a curse.

"I knew it! I knew it! I knew The Captain was no ordinary Captain," someone said.

The others cheered.

"A toast to The Captain, who failed us not!" The Lead Shipman shouted out loud, looking towards me, while the others cheered louder.

The Captain was busy opening an old cask of wine.

"Wine like this, the finest and the rarest, finds you, my friends," he said loudly. "You do not find it."

~

The Cost of Fear

~

There is a price to pay for your fears. And it is no small price.
It is the price of your life itself. It is your life itself.

~

"The path of the Kabbalah needs everything from you, son," The Butcher said to me. "Until you seek the one and only truth of life, I can be of no help to you."

I said nothing.

When I looked within I could see . . . all my longings, all my guilt, all my hurt, and all my dreams, still alive below the pain.

"You must leave now," he said. "And return when truth and self-knowledge is all you seek. For, if there are things you want from yourself or from this world, then go forth into the world and strive for them. You are rested and healthy now."

"I know not what I should do, good sir," I said. "I know not my purpose."

"I cannot tell you what you thirst for, son," he said. "It is you who must look within."

I was quiet.

"Like prayer, peace is of many kinds. And freedom from pain is one such."

I felt a sudden wave of emptiness in my heart. Why I felt so, I could not exactly say.

"Walk free son, walk free," he said. "Choose your life. And stop living like a drifter, like a leaf that can be blown anywhere by any wind. What do you seek beyond peace? Ask yourself every day. And don't stop until you find the answer."

I nodded quietly.

"Just seek that one thing . . . and only that one thing."

~

I do not deliver you. It is you who will deliver yourself.
I have merely placed you on the path.

~

The Pain You Should Welcome

~

There are pains you should welcome, for they are the ones that will deliver you.

~

The Gods We Loved

~

There are Gods who have been slaves of Gods.
They were the Gods who were worshipped for their slavery.

~

There were Gods who stood alone.
So alone, they forgot they even existed.

~

There were Gods who turned silent for a thousand years,
and it passed in a moment.
They were the Gods that played with time.

~

There were Gods that cared for naught.
They were the Gods that could choose to love like no one ever had.

~

There were Gods that got so angry they destroyed the world in a moment.

~

There were Gods that were banished from their own kingdom.

~

And there were Gods who simply walked away.

~

There were Gods who saw their beloved die in their own arms.
There were Gods that brought them to life and gave up their own.

~

There were Gods that wept like you and I could never imagine.
There were Gods who laughed out so loud, it made the whole universe shake.

~

Some say the expansion and contraction of the universe
is a single breath of God.

~

All this you and I will know, my dear.

All this and much more.

~

And the ship sailed through the high skies, where the air was pure but thin. Our lungs struggled a bit at first, but we gradually grew accustomed to it. I could feel the hope in the heart of every shipman now. They waited anxiously to see land.

"Let us make some bows and arrows, my friends, for here, up above in these open skies, we fish for birds," The Captain said out loud. "We need long strings tied to our arrows. Our feathered friends we saw far away from down below will feed us as we travel the skies. I will take you, my friends, not to just any land but a land that you have never seen before."

And the shipmen cheered.

And I closed my eyes. Or were my eyes already half-closed? I wondered.

As I felt the wind on my face, I was unimaginably alone.

~

The Dagger of Truth

~

It was not lies but truth that could destroy a man's life as he knew it.

~

The silence will be unbearable, my son. Every thought and feeling you ever had will fight to live inside you. They will return with a vengeance. But they will pass. And with each passing shall the silence grow.

~

Be patient. For these storms are no ordinary storms. They are your last fight for survival in a battle you have already lost.

~

The Day I Lost My Freedom

~

You will lose your freedom too, my friend. And that will hurt the most. The most.

~

For then you will wait for its return. Endlessly.

~

This shall be your curse and also your blessing. For now you can live neither in chains nor as a free man.

~

This is the time something can be born as never before. As never before.

~

A Life Filled With Regret

~

"This is the only card your mind can play now—guilt and regret. And you alone have the power to call its bluff," The Strange One said to me today. "For it is none other than you who has played it. You are on both sides of this game. You are the one whipping, and you are also the one being whipped."

I heard it all today.

~

The Ones That Never Sleep

~

The eyes of the great ones are always closed, even when open.
And always open, even when closed.
For these are the eyes of the ones that never sleep . . .
The ones that never sleep.

~

The Gospel of Judas

~

"It was in their contract," The Crazy One said. "Judas was told by Jesus to betray Him."

I listened.

"It was His order. It was His will," she continued. "If He was who He was, how could it have been otherwise? After all, God chooses His betrayers as much as He chooses His followers. And His crucifixion as much as His resurrection. He is no victim of circumstance."

And I shed an invisible tear for the burdens we all carried in our ignorance. Even in the face of truth. Even in the face of truth.

~

The Roles We Took Up

~

They are just roles, all of them. Just roles.
And they will have to be played as long as we exist in this world.

~

Take them not too seriously, for they are just roles we play.

~

Yet, make not light of them.
For this role you are playing is exactly what you need.

~

The Promise He Had Made

~

"I will take you there," He had promised, many years ago. "If you let me."

~

I wondered if I had.

~

Not a day passed when I didn't want to jump off the ship and take my chances with the skies.

But I had made a promise to The Captain.

And it was the only thing now that I was living for.

~

BOOK XVI

~

The Endless Journey

~

Never.

"When does this end?"

~

The Rules of Grammar

~

They were the same—the first, the second, and the third person.

The difference lay only in the point of reference.

And that made all the difference.

~

The Ship He Had Already Seen

~

"Do you know what it is you seek, my son?" The Butcher asked him as he was leaving the next morning. He had remembered The Butcher's words about not wasting any time to act, and so he decided to leave the very next morning.

"I seek to find that out, good sir. What it is that I truly want . . ." I replied.

"Then be on your way, son. And stop not until you find your answer," he said. "Remember this when you are tired and weary. For the answer you seek is within yourself, and that can be the most treacherous journey, indeed. The most treacherous."

"I shall remember what you said, good sir."

He replied with a smile so warm, I wondered for a moment if my leaving was the right thing.

"You suffer from hesitation," he said without warning. "Self-doubt is a quality best practiced in balance. Understood?"

"Yes, sir," I said.

"God bless you, son." He smiled. "And be sure to keep warm, for this winter will be a particularly cold one."

~

The Captain's Last Words

~

"Don't jump, my friend," he said. By now I knew that he always knew what I was thinking. Sometimes long before I had even thought it. "You'll find a way to return—I promise you."

I knew I would. For this was truly the home I could never leave.

~

And this was a promise that could not be broken.

~

"Imagine your wildest dreams," he continued. "Now multiply them a thousand times."

I said nothing. I felt nothing. What was there to multiply? I wondered. What was left?

~

A Night at the Tavern

~

"Tonight we shall drink," I said to him, raising my cup of ale and touching his cup. "To friendship," I said aloud.

"To friendship," he repeated, in a softer voice.

And after many a cup, and much laughter, I asked him a question that I had often wondered about but never asked.

"So what really brings you to this village?" I asked. "Surely not to work in a blacksmith's shop."

"I am grateful for my work" he replied.

"But what really brings you here?" I asked again.

He was quiet for a moment. It felt like the right time to tell the truth. "Do you know of a man who died in a forest fire, about fifteen years ago, in this village?"

I paused. Why would a stranger ask me about my father? I wondered. "I do. But why do you ask?"

"I have my reasons," he said.

"You can tell me," I replied. "We are friends, are we not?"

"Yes . . . I have not spoken of this with a soul here," he said. "But if I must, then it should be you." He smiled.

I smiled back.

"You cannot speak of this with anyone," he continued. "Promise me this."

"I promise," I answered.

"You promise on the life of those you love," he said. "On your family."

"Yes," I said immediately. "I do."

"The man who died in the forest fire." He looked straight into my eyes. "He was my father."

~

The Contract We Made

~

"That's impossible," I replied. My mind raced with a thousand thoughts.

"Why do you say that?"

"Because it cannot be."

"It is true, friend. It is true."

"Are you certain of what you say?" I asked.

"Yes." He nodded. "I know this for sure."

"Then we are half-brothers."

~

And the silence that followed may have lasted for lifetimes.

~

We promised never to tell a soul. This would be our secret. And we swore we would take it to our graves. For we both knew in our hearts the reason he had come to this village.

It was for this moment. It was for this very moment.

~

And the ones that followed.

~

But we didn't know that then.

~

Her First Love

~

She knew the day she set eyes on him that he would be the one she would marry. How she knew, she could not say, but she knew it, three years before it happened. She was fifteen then, but she could already see them, exchanging vows, living in a cottage of their own.

She had seen him on the day she had gone to her father's shop one afternoon. He was standing there in the midst of the fires and the coal, tired from the heat and the dirt. But he picked up the hammer once again and beat the red-hot iron bar into a single wedge. He looked up at her, recognizing her for a moment, while she stood silently watching, and then he got back to his work, wiping away the sweat and hair that fell on his forehead. She knew everything in that single glance. She read it in his eyes. Everything.

~

That he was the one.

~

He was the forgotten son.

~

BOOK XVII

~

Inside the Waters

~

Spend enough time with yourself, and you will realize you are God.

~

I am the Holy Spirit. For I am everywhere, and yet nowhere.
I am everything, and yet nothing.

~

"You're still here?" The Madman said, as I opened my eyes to see him floating in front of me.

I was still in the middle of the sea. Dead or alive, I did not know.

~

It all came flashing to me.

~

I had never gone back to the surface. Or the ship.
I was still under the sea.

~

I wasn't ready to die just yet. So I closed my eyes and continued living in my dreams.
And dreams can go on forever. Forever.
Until a part of you decides to wake up.

~

The Captain had not returned. And neither had I.
I had imagined meeting my old friends. I had imagined the ship flying high in the skies. I dreamt it all just as I had wished to dream it.

~

All the clues were there.

I went back and read through the lines I had written in the last few months.

~

"I must go back. I must," I replied. The Madman continued smiling at me.
Page 136

~

There was no struggle to reach the surface, for suddenly I found myself back on the waves, swimming easily toward the ship that I saw sailing in the distance.
Page 137

~

As I got closer to the ship, I could hear the shipmen's voices. Or perhaps I imagined hearing them in anticipation.
Page 137

~

It was obvious.

~

They threw the rope to me, and from the side of the ship, I climbed back to the deck, where I saw for the first time that the shipmen looked different. Or perhaps I had never really noticed them.
Page 137

~

"I wonder who will be the next to leave the ship," he said. "I wonder who will jump."
But those words didn't touch me, even though I heard them. Perhaps they were for someone else.
Whether I had jumped or not, I did not know. But I had returned.
Page 140

~

"*Imagine yourself lying down on a bed, motionless, unable to get up, even though your eyes are open. You know not this, but you are waiting. You are waiting to rise up. And you know not that you are waiting.*"
Page 143

~

I was giving myself clues.

But I wasn't listening.

I wanted to live.

~

The story was perfect as it was.
It was just me who was missing.
Page 147

~

What is hidden in this book remains hidden, my friend.
Even from you, even from you.
Until you find it.
Until you find it for yourself.
Page 167

~

I wondered what else was still hidden from me.

~

Truly, I saw nothing and felt nothing, for my senses were no longer connected to my heart and mind. And I could feel, since I had returned to
the ship, that nothing was being remembered, either. The past was clear.
It was my present that was blurry.

Page 151

~

Our bodies felt disconnected from our selves. It was indeed a strange time.

Page 169

~

Naturally.

~

Journal of a Dying Man

~

A free man is not one who has no past or future,
but one who is bound by neither.

~

"I will see you on the other side," I had told her.

"Yes—see you on the other side," she had replied.

We didn't know exactly what that meant. But we meant what we said.

~

"I promise you not life but death," He had said, a long time ago.

And in my heart, I knew He was speaking the truth. He would deliver me right to the door. For if there was anyone who could, it was He.

I knew that without a doubt.

Without a doubt.

~

This was not a book I was writing. It was my journal.

~

It was the journal of a dying man.

~

For what else would a dying man do but look back upon his whole life . . . and imagine the ones he had loved before? So that he could make his peace with them . . . all those he had loved and all those who had loved him.

~

He remembered them all. Every single one of them . . . including the ones who believed they had forgotten him—and the ones who believed they'd been forgotten.

They were all a part of him now.

And everything that had happened was in the contract.

And everything had gone exactly according to plan.

~

Everything.

~

After all, God made no mistakes.

~

BOOK XVIII

~

The End of the Path

~

He was helpless. For there was nothing he could do. There was no turning back now. He would be here in the middle of the sea, beneath the waters, on the ocean bed, for as long as he needed to. Neither dead nor alive. For as long as God willed him to be.

~

And nothing was in his hands. Nothing.

~

And the paragraphs were shorter now. Just like the chapters.

Everything was rushing.

~

The Man Who Lived Inside Me

~

"Sacrifice is a noble thing. It is the noblest of things," I heard my mind say to me. But clearly this was not the truth. It's just what I had believed for years, perhaps lifetimes.

~

"We do things for others. Not for ourselves. We are born to serve, after all, are we not?" it continued. For the first time, I heard the man inside me who had held me hostage ever since I could remember.

~

"Happiness and freedom—they are momentary, passing. Life is a struggle, a test. It is the way of life."

~

"We must do our duty. For duty is what grounds us and gives our lives purpose."

~

"And you who fail in your duty will be left with the blood of betrayal on your hands. You will. And this blood will never wash away. Never."

~

"The greatest sin is to lie to another."

~

"Those who live with shame in their hearts are the ones closer to me. For every man and woman must carry the burden of their own sins."
It could appear that it was being spoken by the voice of God Himself.

~

"I am the all-powerful, all-forgiving God. And you are the sinner who must pay for his sins to enter my kingdom."

~

"You pay when you carry the burden of your sins. You pay when you serve others. You pay when you sacrifice. You pay when you repent. You pay when you fall at my feet and beg for forgiveness. And you pay when you abandon the pleasures of life and turn your attention toward me."

~

But when would the balance be cleared? I wondered. A self-imposed debt could never be paid back. Never. Until I released myself from it.

~

It was I who held the key to the kingdom of heaven.

~

It was a false god that I had believed—one who had entered my blood and taken my soul hostage. And he made me suffer, one way or another, and then indulge in pleasures in order to escape from this burden. And pay for those sins. And so on and so forth. It was an endless cycle.

~

The Greatest Actor Ever Born

~

"Be the best at what you do. Become untouchable. Be a genius. Otherwise, you are a loser . . . a failure."

~

There were so many ways we held ourselves hostage. So many ways. And life was innocent, like the red squirrels I saw every day in this beautiful country, hopping and jumping. They danced from tree to tree without a care in the world.

~

Seriousness was a disease that we all inherited, whether we liked it or not. Whether we invited it or not.

It was in our blood now. And it would not allow peace and joy to spring from our hearts.

~

"Happiness for no reason at all . . . That's a sign of madness, insanity."

~

There was no beating him. He had everything covered. Everything.

~

"Live a frugal life. Be humble in your ways. For those who are meek are closest to my heart."

~

He could fool anyone. He could use the words of the great ones to suit his agenda. He was the greatest actor ever born.

~

The Story of Love

~

Love was sometimes returned. And sometimes refused.
And sometimes, it was just accepted.

~

And I was grateful for whatever was the case. For we were all promised nothing when we came onto this Earth. Nothing. It was all a gift.
All of it.

~

"Let the celebrations begin," the blacksmith had said that evening. "The time has come to eat and be grateful for all that we are receiving. For this is the wedding feast that marks the beginning of a new life. May you both love each other through the challenges you will no doubt face as you grow up in this world, which is as benevolent as it is unforgiving." He smiled as he looked at the newly wedded couple. "I trust you will love my daughter as much as I have loved her, if not more. May nothing come between your love."

"You have my word, sir," my brother replied.

And the songsters began playing their music.

~

The Wine That Never Left Our Blood

~

He had walked many miles, spending the night under the trees or in empty barns that were no longer in use. And every night before he went to sleep, he prayed to God to help him find his way. It was a simple prayer, of the first or perhaps the second kind, for he was asking something for himself. And though he was grateful for everything The Butcher had taught him, this knowledge also made him weary. It was a long journey—too long. And what could he ever find with so much weariness in his heart, he wondered . . . as his eyes closed and he drifted into sleep.

~

The next day, he walked on, with a smile in his heart and hope for the future. Perhaps prayers did work after all, he thought, climbing over the hill as the

215

*light of the sun faded. He could see, from there, the dim lights of the old port
at a distance.*

~

*It was a full-moon night, sometime in December. And the winds that blew
over the sea and into the port between the ships stung his face like an arctic
breeze. He saw it there. The ship. It was old but strong. Like a partly wrinkled man
who still had many good years ahead of him. And on top of the upper deck sat
The Captain, proudly, with a cup in one hand.*

~

I knew everything the moment I set eyes on Him. Everything. Except how
it would actually end.

~

"Get aboard, young lads, if you want to take a journey you will be certain to
forget. You will see lands you have only dreamt of and swim with fish so beautiful
you will forget about the women here on land." He smiled wickedly and stroked
his beard with pride. "And the wine that lies in the casks at the bottom of this
ship has been made from the finest of grapes, I can assure you. They are the
oldest and finest wines you will ever taste."

I was the first to get aboard that night. The drunkards all came aboard, too,
for the promise of good wine was enough for them. "I had plenty of women in my
time. From the youngest to the oldest. From the most beautiful to the ugliest," one
strong-looking lad laughed and said, as he hopped aboard and stood at the bridge
shouting out to the others who stood around, curiously listening to The Captain.
"Get on board, my friends, get on board! Enough with your miserable lives!"

"What will you pay us?" A leper, hardly fit to be a shipman, asked The Captain.

"What you deserve, my lad, exactly what you deserve," he replied with a wink, while he made a head count of all those aboard the ship. "But do have a cup of wine before you make your final decision, my friends."

And the wine flowed, and the men assembled quickly. "One hundred and thirty-six, sire," The Leper chimed in, before The Captain could ask.

~

Bits and Pieces

~

And it was from the very first sip of the warm ruby wine that we were changed.

~

The wine, the wine!

~

It was the wine that The Captain had kept fueling us with that day . . . which had made us all forget . . .

~

We would lose our dearest memories. We would wipe our minds and hearts clean. We would forget it all, the happiness and the pain. We would remember nothing about ourselves. Until the day we were supposed to. In bits and pieces. Until the day we were supposed to.

~

We had sat on the banks of the river that passed a few miles away from our village. It was evening, and the last rays of the red sun fell across the skies, touching the bottom of the clouds above.

"Say something," I had said, holding her hands. "I promise I won't hold you to your words."

We were quiet for a minute.

"You are free to say anything. It's only for this moment. Just this moment."

"I love you," she said, knowing that those were the words I wanted to hear. Whether they were true or not, I didn't care.

~

The Holy Dagger

~

The silver dagger is no ordinary dagger. For it frees both the one it pierces and the one who holds it.

~

Be warned, those who pick up this dagger. Be warned.

~

The Last Door

~

Only when all the doors outside are closed will you enter the kingdom
that lies within you.

~

A Wish Is All You Need

~

Make a wish, my friends. Make it with an innocent heart. And be patient. For
as long as we live in this body, time doth have its hold on us. But not for long.
As your wish is none other than mine. And together,
we can make all our dreams come true.

~

BOOK XIX

~

The New Commandments

~

You shall not find peace and happiness unless all around you are happy,
for even if you know it not, they are a part of you.

~

You shall not find peace and happiness until you realize all men and women
are your very own brothers and sisters.

~

You shall not find peace and happiness until you realize that the anger and hate
you carry in your heart is for yourself, and therefore yours to release.

~

You shall not find peace and happiness until you live your truth,
which must come from an innocent heart.

~

You shall not find peace and happiness until you begin to laugh at yourself,
even when things are difficult.

~

You shall not find peace and happiness by pleasing others. Just like you,
they must find it for themselves.

~

You shall not find peace and happiness by harming others,
for they are a part of you, even if you know it not.

~

You shall not find peace and happiness in any one thing or any person,
no matter who or what it may be. For that which does not include
all can never deliver you.

~

You shall not find peace and happiness in the health of your body.
For your body will fail you, today or tomorrow.

~

You shall not find peace and happiness in greed and pettiness, for they are both the fruits of your lacking, which is none but a trick of the mind.

~

You shall not find peace and happiness until you begin to share of yourself and all the gifts you have been blessed with.

~

You shall not find peace and happiness by serving the less fortunate. You are free to do so, once you have found your own treasures within.

~

You shall not find peace and happiness until you learn to be patient, for good things are always coming to those who wait with a smile.

~

They came one after another, without a break, as I struggled to type the words as fast as I could. And each line I wrote pierced my own heart as never before.

~

You cannot find peace and happiness until you make your heart innocent again.

~

I knew that was the last one. I could feel it in my heart and in my breath . . .
For I could breathe easily now.

~

And I sat down to pray to the Lord.

~

It was of the fourth kind.

~

Exactly as The Butcher had spoken.

~

BOOK XX

~

The Empty Vessel

~

Innocence is emptiness, for truly it seeks nothing and wants nothing for itself.

~

The Silence That Never Ends

~

This is what the great ones spoke about. This was the silence that never ends.

~

As I looked out of my window, over the snow-covered hills and peaks that surrounded the valley, I could see the sun, almost hidden by the clouds and the mist. But its rays streamed down below, like a crown of light just above the top of the mountain. It was an unforgettable sight—as if God had Himself shone through for a moment to greet me on that cold winter morning.

~

The lord shines on the righteous and the sinners alike
but lives in the hearts of the innocent.

~

The Angels That Watch Over Us

~

They are angels, those who never stop loving you, no matter what.
They are your angels.

~

They are angels, those who see your innocence. Who see you as you truly are.
They are your angels.

~

They live here on Earth and in the world beyond.

~

They feel your pain when you cry, even when you cannot.
Especially when you cannot.

~

And they smile when they know you are happy.

~

They are your angels.

~

Learn to see, learn to see.

~

The Day I Died

~

Was it the day I fell into the water?

~

Or the day I stopped breathing?

~

Or the day I was told I would fall one day?

~

Or the day I realized I was dead?

~

Or the day I realized there was no coming back to the surface?

~

Or the day I knew I could never die?

~

Which was that day?

~

The Inherited Doctrines

~

Riches hold hostage the heart of both the miser and the spendthrift,
for both believe in its false promises.

~

The last error always hurts the most. That is why it becomes the last.

~

The Glory of Love

~

*When you are without all hope . . . not even the last hope that hope will return
someday into your heart . . . it is then that you will realize you need it not.*

~

*We are free, we are free. You shall proclaim. And the only one who will listen to
those words will be me. For, only the Infinite one can hear the voice
of the eternal. Only the Infinite one.*

~

*Love is not for the weak. It is a privilege for those
who have stopped waiting for it.*

~

*We fight for it. To the ends of the earth we go in search of it.
But never must we destroy ourselves or others for it.*

~

The true lover is one who has put down all arms forever.

~

Love demands, and Love delivers. Let it never be said that Love has failed. It demands, and delivers, to those who truly love.

~

When love fails, remember that it is you who failed yourself. Not I. For I am Love, infinitely strong in my weakness and infinitely patient in my impatience.

~

I am the shattered soul that lives in the dust and in the skies.

~

Find yourself, and you will find me. Become me, and you shall find yourself. For I am Love. I am Love.

~

At the Bottom of the Sea

~

There, at the bottom of the sea, in what felt like the most beautiful place on Earth now, something arose in my heart. Something like love. But bigger and wider.

Here, it made no difference whether I closed my eyes or kept them open. For it was all the same deep, dark blue everywhere, and the glowfish twinkled like thousands of little stars in a clear night sky.

~

I wished I could have written down what was in my heart at that moment. But it was impossible. Leave alone words . . . even feelings weren't enough.

~

The only thing that could be written down was a song that appeared in my heart.

~

There Once Was a Captain

~

There once was a Captain
Who was neither alive nor dead.

There once was a Captain,
Who listened to things he himself said.

There once was a Captain,
Who dreamt of a world, unlike the one we had earned.

There once was a Captain,
Who came to destroy all that we had learned.

There once was a Captain,
Who was always tired but never weary.

There once was a Captain
Who turned the wheel, even when it wasn't easy.

There once was a Captain,
as great as God, and as human as you.

There once was a Captain,
who could will our dreams into coming true.

There once was a Captain,
Who tightened the chains around our feet.

He did it in plain sight,
For us all to see.

It was all part of the design,
Some strange methodology.

There once was a Captain,
He was called the King of the Sea.

There once was a Captain,
He was called the King of the Sea.

~

BOOK XXI

~

The Last Revolution

~

This is the only revolution, my friend, the one that starts from within.
For even the ones with riches beyond imagination cannot buy their way in.

And even you who wish to forsake everything for your place,
Must wait in patience for the right time and space.

That unspeakable treasure was always inside,
It knew it would find you, how long would you hide.

This will be the first and last revolution that took place,
For everything that ever happened, was an imagined fall from grace.

Nothing can be said that you have not already heard,
For you will be both the one who delivers and the delivered.

~

And Nothing Ever Happened

~

"The time has come, my friend, to make a choice," The Captain said, in my head. I was silent.

"Either dream your dream, and I shall dream it with you," he said. "Or dream my dream . . ."

I said nothing.

"Are you ready to stay under the ocean forever? Or are you thirsty for air?"

~

Remember, there are no right or wrong answers. But just one that feels close to your heart. As if it were always so, even though it appears you are choosing it now.

~

And I knew my truth.

~

And I came to the surface, not effortlessly, but somehow, despite my flagging arms and legs. I saw the ship sailing quietly, just as I had dreamt how it would happen. I wondered if The Captain would be there or not, even though my heart said he would be standing in his customary place, on the top of the upper deck.

~

And when I reached the ship, I saw that, sure enough, he was.

~

"You were in your cabin, I know," I said, when I saw him come toward me, while the shipmen cheered on.

The Captain smiled at me but said nothing.

"Are we ready to fly now?" I said to him. The others thought I was speaking in metaphors.

"We certainly are," he said. "You made the right choice."

I wondered what it was, for most important choices are made a moment before you actually make them. They happen in a place that is as sacred as it is hidden.

~

And we flew through the air just as I had imagined it. The shipmen cheering . . . The Captain, holding his cup of wine, announcing his plans and schemes to the shipmen. And I, silently watching the scene unfolding . . . as I had watched it once before, under the sea. But something was different. The green-eyed boy was nowhere to be seen.

~

He is blessed who walks naked on this earth,
Holding naught in his hands, carrying naught in his heart.
He shall find the kingdom of heaven,
for we are but together, and even death cannot us part.

~

BOOK XXII

~

The Shiva Principle

~

I walk with the disappeared.
I run with the wind.
I play with God.
I swim in sand.

I drink poison in wine glasses.
I eat the dirt of the land,
I bathe in the milk of forces.
One day you will understand.

I cry for souls.
I weep for your fears.
I find my heaven.
In saltless tears.

I dance with all.
All dance with me.

You, too, are dancing,
Even if you cannot see.

I measure none.
I stand tall.
None are below me,
For I am one and all.

~

Just because you don't believe in my God doesn't mean I won't believe in yours. You see . . . I see Him everywhere.

Everywhere.

~

My willingness to destroy what is not you is as great as my love for you.

~

BOOK XXIII

~

The Book of Forgiveness

~

*Forgive the land that stood silent beneath you while you waged wars
and drew blood that was all in vain.
Forgive the trees that stood still while you hung your enemies
and those who believed differently from you.
Forgive the sea while it watched its waves destroy the homes
and families of the innocent.
Forgive yourself for all the pain you caused and all the pain you are yet to.
To others. But mostly yourself.
Forgive yourself for watching silently.
And forgive God for watching silently.
There was no other way.
For You are but His child. Created in His image. Created with His power.
Created with His compassion.
And He lives as You today.
So forgive us both, once and for all.
And be free.*

~

I am you, finding myself, discovering what happiness is and what I want.
I am you, ignoring my own cries of pain as I destroy the lives of others.
I am you, stubborn in my foolishness and adamant in my knowledge.
I am you, the one who will not give up until the last drop of blood is fallen.
I am you, the one looking for peace now.
I am you, the one who will not be able to forgive himself today.
This is my journey, too.

~

See through yourself.
See through yourself.

~

BOOK XXIV

~

The Day of Release

~

"You really don't want to be here, do you?" The Captain asked me suddenly that evening as I sat watching the sunset in the distance.

"I do," I said. "Where else do I have to go?"

"That's no answer." His voice was louder now.

"But . . ." I tried to reply.

"Enough," he said. And he pushed me over the edge of the ship that was more my home than it had ever been.

~

What just happened? I wondered. This couldn't be happening.

~

It is. It is. I am falling.

~

Life never waits, my friend. Never.

~

Fear not.

~

And I fell through the air, over the clouds and the mountains, towards the ground.

~

Watch. Watch.
Resist all conclusions.

~

There was nothing I could do.
And the song played once again in my head . . .

~

There once was a Captain,
You may never believe.

And I was the chosen one,
Once upon a time, you see.

There once was a Captain,
Who could do no wrong.

There once was a Captain,
I called him the King of the Sea.

~

On the Way to Heaven

~

As I fell through the sky, I saw around me the light of a thousand suns. I saw fish that leapt like giant waves. And I saw the sky in all the colors that I had ever seen in my life. As I tumbled, I saw flashes of the snow-capped mountains, standing majestically, watching in silence as life passed by. I saw lakes that were a deep cobalt blue, like the eyes of a rare white beast that no one had ever seen. The air was cold, and my face tingled as the moist air carried me.

~

I could feel my heart beating fast inside my chest, for I knew it would be a matter of moments before I would fall to the ground. I could feel my head becoming heavy with anticipation. And my stomach churned as if I were about to vomit.

~

How many deaths would one die before dying? I wondered . . . tumbling again and again until there was no up and no down. No life and no death. No sky and no earth. All that remained was the throbbing beat of my heart, loud like thunder.

~

The Day I landed

~

And suddenly, amidst the mountain peaks and a small patch of green grass, I landed. Lightly, on my feet, as if God had slowed down time just that very moment in order for me to live.

~

I didn't know where I was. But I was on land. And even though I had been here before, all that existed were pictures in my mind, not memories. For memories lived in our hearts, but mine was empty of everything. Land felt different this time. As if the whole Earth held me in her strong but delicate hands.

~

I saw the rising sun, its light slowly spreading its rays across the fluffy white clouds. And a single fading star in the morning sky to point me the way forward.

~

BOOK XXV

~

The Moments Before Death

~

But who knew whether I had truly landed or not . . .

When your mind doesn't know how to deal with reality, it fast-forwards itself into a happy future. It glosses over the present.

And pretends that nothing ever happened. It had happened once before. But this time, I caught myself.

This time I would face what had to be faced.

~

There was no easy way to make friends with death. For death was just like the truth. It would destroy everything in its wake.

~

The Great Purge

~

"I don't want to see you in this life," He screamed. Those were His last words. "You have a disorder, a sickness. You have some weird concept of love, which is not love at all. That's why you will die alone in this life. I've had enough of you. Enough. Get out of my life. Get yourself treated."

~

And as I wrote the words I never wanted to hear or write down, they rang harder in my ears than anything ever had till now.

~

I had believed that whatever I did was free from blame.

Because it was always He that did everything.

~

It was not me. It was He . . . I had told myself, many times.

~

But this was not the truth.

~

It was always me.

~

January 31, 2014

~

The Book of Truth

~

Sometimes, when love leaves a man's heart, all that's left is a memory of beauty that he wants to capture somehow. Anyhow . . .

To make his soul whole again.

~

But nothing worked.

~

Everything I had written felt like a lie. Like little bits of truth, held together by my imagination and a string of lies that I had to tell myself in order to exonerate myself from all that I had done.

I had meshed together all that had happened with all that I imagined had happened. And in my story, I was the chosen one. The one who was blameless, the one who was free from consequence.

~

Yes, I was the chosen one.

I was the one chosen by life to see the truth of myself, if I so wished. If I so wished.

~

But we all were . . . the chosen ones.

~

If we so wished.

~

We all wanted to dream. That's what we were all told. Dream a dream grand and large. Follow your heart. Live for your dream. But what they didn't say was that any dream that begins with your eyes closed would soon turn into a nightmare.

~

And the day of reckoning was close. The great sea of seas was coming. It always was. At our doorstep.

It was we who closed our eyes and began to dream, the moment truth, like the cold, icy water, could even touch the bottom of our feet.

~

Not this time, I said to myself. *Not this time.*

~

All the Things I Saw

~

"Get out of my life, God!" I screamed silently. "I don't want you anywhere around me—you understand?"

Tears of anger.

"I will live with myself now. Go find something better to do," I continued. "Soon all this, including me, will be gone, and our fight will be over.'

Bloodshot eyes.

"Until then, leave me alone. Just leave me alone."

~

And just because I got no answer didn't mean He wasn't listening to me.

~

I knew He was. I could feel Him silently watching, without a whisper or a sound.

~

He would do nothing now. Just watch.

I could scream, shout, beg, or yell. I would, I knew. But it would make no difference. None at all.

For there was no redemption, no punishment, and no salvation on offer. It never was.

~

The Point of No Return

~

I looked outside my window to see the snowflakes swirl and fall across the streets and the trees. It would be a long and cold winter, I knew. And the more tightly I clenched my fists the harder the landing would be.

~

The time had come to watch life silently unfold. The time had come to keep my hands open this time. With my palms facing the sky. And my eyes wide open so I wouldn't slip into a dream.

~

BOOK XXVI

~

The Gathering of the Innocent

~

Time may have laid its net for you. But so did I lay my net for the innocent.
To be captured. For this will be the largest gathering of the innocent.
And it is I who shall deliver them.

~

The Art of Capture

~

The only art to be learned is love. For it is love that captures one and all. No
one will be spared. And none of the innocent, undelivered.

~

The Fools of the World

~

Real knowledge is always bestowed, never learned.

~

The highest truths demand great humility. Not will or intelligence.

~

And Vengeance Shall Be Mine

~

He gave up the part for the whole.

~

But I was the part. And he was my father.

~

He gave up his life so that others may live.

~

But what about me?

~

How do you take vengeance on life, your absent father, God, and Him, when they all seem to have forgotten you?

Simple.

You take it out on yourself. You allow yourself to sink into a place so dark and bereft of any light, so that they writhe in pain. Along with you.

~

And they did cry. Along with me, they did.

~

But I never heard them.

For you cannot hear what you do not want to hear.

~

I sought vengeance. And vengeance would be mine. At any cost.
At any cost.

~

But one day, I knew . . . I would be free.

~

Somewhere down the line. Somewhere in the future.
But not today.

Today, pain was the order of the day.

~

And he asked forgiveness from all those he had caused pain to.

For a man who brings pain upon himself can do no better for others. Even if he wishes to. Even if he wishes to.

~

This was the truth.

~

I was the perpetrator, the victim, the judge, and the convict of my own life.

~

The Silent Verses

~

The House of Cards

~

Love's New Beginnings

~

The New Imagined Future

~

No Cause for Celebration

~

The Speechless Heart

~

A Life Without Tests

~

The Creation of Purpose

~

The Fruitless Tree

~

The Granter of Unspoken Wishes

~

The Day Everything Would Be Lost

~

It wasn't here yet, the sea of seas. It was still coming. And the mind's only way of dealing with this truth was to pretend that it had already come and gone.

~

But I knew this now.

~

And it wasn't about possessions or relationships or my body. It was knowing that not a single thought or belief I had ever had was absolutely true. And not a single feeling I had ever felt would last forever.

~

And that would change my relationship to myself forever.

~

I Am

~

I am a traveler with no place to go.

I am a teacher with nothing to teach.

I am a songster with no song to sing.

I am my breath, breathing me.

I am.

~

Song of the Sea

~

As I fell, I wondered if I would see The Captain again.
How would I keep my promise when there was no one to keep my promise to?

~

A Thousand Deaths

~

Come, my love.
Let us die a thousand deaths.

Let us leap from cliffs.
Let us burn in the fires.

Come, my love.
Let us die a thousand deaths.

Cry till our eyes dry up.
Drown in our loneliness.

Come, my love.
Let us die a thousand deaths.

Drink in our imagined lives.
Swallow our dreams alive.

Come, my love.
Let us die a thousand deaths.

We've lived long enough.

Let us leave our selves behind.

Come, my love.

Come with me.

Come, my love.

Hold on tight.

~

BOOK XXVII

~

Round and Round

~

We all circled around a funnel infinitely. Until the day we were ready to fall in and see what was on the other side. This was the abyss. Da'at. The black hole that took everything in.

~

And the moment you fell in was the moment when you came out the other side.

~

That's what I imagined.

~

The Living Multi-verse

~

We weren't living in a multi-verse. We were the living multi-verse. For we were all the same God, the same One, like two drops from the same ocean, living different lives, each of us in our own universe, believing that we were separate.

~

The Impossible Dream

~

Since I was a child, the question would come back to me from time to time . . .

Why did I find myself here . . . within this body. Why was my point of reference located here and not there . . . inside you, looking through your eyes?

For it was not my choice that I found myself in here, in this body that I then started calling my own.

~

And now, I had lived long enough within this body, within this person. Now I wanted to live everywhere but within the confines of myself.

~

But impossible dreams had no pathways.

~

The Real Story

~

It was I. The one who was mad. The one who had stayed on the ship too long. It was I who could climb to the top of the mast.

After all, it was I who spoke with myself. It was I who heard voices speaking in strange dialects.

~

It was obvious now.

~

But today, as I realized this, another truth was seen. I was also The Leper who was angry with The Captain for leading us nowhere. But who still waited to be called upon some day. I was also The Winemaker, who kept up the spirits of all on the ship. And I was also The Lead Shipman, who lived for one thing and one thing only—The Captain. It was me The Captain had spoken to the night before he disappeared. And the boy with the green eyes was also me, the younger me. He was the part of me that still hoped for the promised land . . . the part in me that I could no longer see in myself.

~

The Voice had told me a long time ago. "You will fail, one way or another. You have to." But I still had a promise to keep.

And so The Lead Shipman stayed on the ship with The Captain, while I fell through the skies, still in search of a dream or in the hope of somehow fulfilling my promise to The Captain.

And the ship sailed through the air silently and steadily, without me.

~

Who Was I?

~

And suddenly I realized that I was no longer The Lute Player.

~

He was gone.

~

And I was no longer The Madman, who struggled to make sense of a life that made no sense.

~

And in that moment I knew nothing.
Nothing at all.

~

The Sign of Four

~

And suddenly I remembered The Captain's words from a long time ago, when he was drunk from many a cup of wine, "Eliminate the impossible . . . and whatever remains . . ." he had muttered. And I had wondered why The Captain would quote Sherlock Holmes. But that was what he had said, so I wrote it down and forgot all about it.

Until today, when I remembered it as clear as a whistle.

~

". . .when you have eliminated the impossible, then whatever remains, however improbable, must be the truth."
Sherlock Holmes, The Sign of Four, *by Sir Arthur Conan Doyle*

~

I was still missing something.

~

BOOK XXVIII

~

The Man Who Gave Up

~

As I fell, I saw on my left the gentle hills that looked familiar, as if I had seen them before, not long ago.

~

"Find out what you truly want," The Butcher had said before I left the village. And I remembered I had embarked on a journey to find out what the purpose of my life was.

~

"I can give it to you," He said, in my dreams, as He often would. "Absolute freedom. But do you really want it? You will have to leave yourself behind."
I had no answer. And I hated myself for that.
One day I would, I thought to myself, as I awoke. One day I would.

~

I remembered the words of the King when I had left. "Come back when you are tired of traveling."

~

"I will send you far away from me," The Voice had said.

~

"You began your journey where I ended mine," I heard my father say. "You are the continuation of me, and therefore there could never be any fight between me and you, other than the one you imagined."

~

And The Captain stood silent at the front of the deck, watching the clear blue skies above, the vast seas below, and the speckled clouds at a distance, knowing that everything was moving beautifully, like clockwork, and nothing was out of place.

~

I knew nothing now. Except one thing. That He was the King. He was The Captain who never made a mistake. And that once upon a very long time, I was the chosen one.

~

BOOK XXIX

~

The Sacrifice We Never Made

~

"What can you give your life for?" The King had asked me, a long time ago.

"Anything." I had replied. But it was a lie. The truth was that I wasn't ready to give my life for a single thing. I wanted to live.

It was pain that I wanted to be free from.

~

The Burning Fields

~

The day you truly want to know yourself, stripped bare of all that is false,
is the day you shall know me.
That is the day I shall reveal myself.

~

The Legacy of Judas

~

There was a verse you wrote . . . a thousand deaths . . .
Read it again.
That was not from you to your beloved, son.
That was from Me to You.

~

The Captured Pretender

~

Stop calling yourself by the names that were given to you.
And stop calling me by names you gave me.

~

The Origins of Sirius

~

Death is a greater truth than life, for that is the place where you come from,
and that is the place you will return to. Death is infinite. Embrace it.

~

*Everything happened just a moment ago. And everything that is to happen
will happen just a moment later.*

~

*Be free from time. Be free from this body.
And be free from your thoughts and feelings.
Be free.*

~

Who was speaking? I asked myself again and again. But no answer came.

~

Who are you? I asked.

~

*I am that from which all arises and into which all disappears.
I am everything. And I am nothing.
I am what you need to hear so that you can go where you want to go.
I am your imagination. And I am the truth.
I am your mind, and I am that which will destroy your mind.
I am the snake eating its own tail.*

~

I am The Voice of Prayer.

I am *The Voice of Truth.*
I am *The Voice of the Path.*

~

But truly, I am you.

~

I am You. Not you as you believe yourself to be, but you as you really are.

~

Truly, You are Me.

~

Truly, I am You?

~

Yes.

~

Everything you have written so far was not you talking to yourself.

~

It was me talking to myself.

~

BOOK XXX

~

The Wrong Door

~

It's the only door I can lead you to.
Anywhere else, you will have to walk yourself.
For I know, more than anyone else, that no one can take you there.
And no one can open that door but you.

~

The Grand Delusion

~

That which speaks cannot speak to that which is speaking. It's impossible.

~

If you want to understand the absolute, it is impossible.
The part cannot see the whole. Only the whole can see the part.

~

Where do you stand?

~

The Game of Chess

~

You knew the whole game even before it began, didn't you?
(silence)

~

You knew every move even before it was played, didn't you?
(silence)

~

I was chosen, to lose, not win, wasn't I?
(silence)

~

I haven't fully accepted defeat, have I?
(silence)

~

I still hope for the day we are side by side, don't I?

(*silence*)

~

But that day is never coming, is it?

(*silence*)

~

It makes no difference when I let go of the ship, does it?

(*silence*)

~

The Truth of the Matter

~

I was lost without The Captain. Completely and utterly lost.

~

But there was no going back.

~

This event had to be faced. Head on.

~

There's always a moment when you know you can't look back. It doesn't come often. But when it does, you know it.

~

Fear and panic strikes your heart, and you feel a terror that can only be lived, never described.

v

It's like falling into a black hole and knowing you won't ever come out.

~

You don't feel like God. You feel like death.

~

And there's absolutely nothing you can do about it.
Absolutely nothing.

~

And, strangely, that is exactly what gives you faith as you tumble through the darkness.

~

You cannot experience an event that extends beyond your existence.
It's simply not possible.

~

BOOK XXXI

~

The Great Void

~

He was at the bottom of the ocean forever.

~

There were no two possibilities.
There never were.

~

"I never asked you what you would die for. I asked you what you could give your life for," The King said, smiling.

~

Song for the Hopeless

~

"Destroy a man's future, and he will die of insanity. Strip him of illusions, and he will shrivel up like a dry seed and forever be lost to the world."

~

The words echoed through the hills, the valleys, and the oceans.

~

Unless that's what he chooses. And knows that he chooses.

In which case, he would be free.

~

The Invisible Bloodlines

~

And as he descended upon the undulating hills, the trees carried a familiar smell. It was as if the whole Earth held him like a feather in her strong but soft hands. And in a moment, he realized that he wasn't far away from the village where he had grown up.

He remembered his mother's words, "You'll be back," as he drifted through the gentle landscape. The cottages looked beautiful in their stillness, and the trees and the bushes remained as silent as ever, even as they swayed to the cool breeze. And when he looked up at the clouds, it was as if they, too, had formed into shapes that he had seen before.

He felt like a child again.

~

As he looked on, there was no one he could actually recognize. It had been a long time. Still, they looked like family, like people he had grown up with . . . He reached the house—the house that was home and also the one that reminded him he was always a stranger. And before he could knock on the door, a young girl who looked no more than twelve opened it.

"Hello, dear," he wanted to say.

She ran out into the front yard.

He went in, looking around the house that looked quite different from what he remembered.

Only the fireplace looked the same.

~

And when he entered the kitchen, he saw her cooking.

But when he looked closer, it wasn't her. She had the same slender nose, the same brown hair, and the same eyes.

"Violet, come back here, and eat your lunch." Her voice echoed through the walls.

And the little girl came running back into the house.

~

He saw a letter on the table.

And he knew it all at once.

~

That's how things are known . . . I thought to myself.

~

It was the year fifteen hundred and seventy-six.

~

Everyone was gone. Including me.

~

Into the future and into the past,
Backwards and forwards,
Until eternity becomes your eternal truth.
And you are one with your eternal self.

~

And there was no way to get back to a past that no longer existed.

~

Did she and my brother live a happy life?
Did she love me?
Did I love her?
Did I jump off the ship, or had the ship released me?
Would I ever meet The Captain again?
How old was I?

Where was I?

~

There were a thousand questions.

But there were no answers. The only thing that remained was the silent hum I felt in my heart.

~

I am the one I called Sirius. I am everywhere and nowhere.
I cannot die because I was always alive.
I cannot be found, for I am everywhere. I cannot be lost, for I am everywhere.

~

Everything you see is you. Everything you touch is you.
Everything you destroy is you. Everything you love is you.
Love is eternal. As am I. As are you.

~

Remember this.
For what you remember in your heart is more important
than what you will ever do. Or can do.

~

And suddenly, as I looked at Violet's smiling face, I could see in her eyes a little bit of him, a little bit of her, and even a little bit of myself. She was my grand-niece after all. We were all there, alive in her soul.

Was she smiling at me? Could she see me? *I wondered.*

~

"Do you like reading?" I asked a seven-year-old girl I had met for the first time.

"Yes," she said shyly.

"I'm writing a book, you know."

"What's it about?"

"It's about love, a boy on a ship, and a Captain."

"Does it have a happy ending?"

"Many," I said. "But some sad ones, too."

~

Without warning, she put her arms around me, and kissed my cheek, staring at me with a blank look on her face.

I was completely overwhelmed. A strange sense of joy mixed with enormous sadness surged through my body.

It was as if one of Gods own angels had kissed me.

And I knew I would never forget that moment.

~

BOOK XXXII

~

The Book That Cannot Be Written

~

"I don't tell you what to do," He had said clearly one night, years ago. "I tell you what you will do, sooner or later." And He smiled.

~

You need nothing. Not from anyone. Especially not from yourself.
The time has come to give. And so you shall. And so you shall.

~

When you are tired and weary, take refuge in your silence.

~

You are free to do as you please. And you are completely bound by what must be done.

~

Don't fight me. You cannot win. For truly, I am you, and you will be fighting the impossible battle.

~

Keep smiling. In your heart. Deep in your heart.

~

She found the book in a dusty old cupboard that hadn't been opened for years. She was a young girl but an old soul. And little did she know, as she blew the dust from the musty cover, that books as ancient as this could tell her as much about her future as they did about her history and the unspoken question in her heart that not even she knew she had inherited.

After all, real bloodlines could weave their way through the faintest traces of blood—and sometimes even without them.

They were invisible. But the only thing that was real for those who could see them.

~

Who was this? I didn't know.

~

But she would. She would.

~

For something to happen, time matters. But for nothing,
a thousand years or a single moment are both the same.

~

The Answer That Had No Question

~

"Unhappiness will not lead you there," He had said. And it was one line of His that I never forgot. "When you are tired of happiness, that's when you know you are at the door."

~

It is not traveling that brings you closer to your destination. It is what you seek
with your whole heart that finds you, wherever you may be.

~

Locate yourself.

I . . . I cannot.

~

Identify yourself.

I cannot.

~

The vast emptiness could be unbearable at times.

~

What do you want?

I cannot . . .

~

Who are you?

I . . .

~

I said, what do you want?

I can't do this anymore.

~

The ship was light as a feather that day as it flew through the skies like a bird in the wind.

~

BOOK XXXIII

~

The Trail of Broken Promises

~

". . . all our struggles, all in vain . . . we were already dead the moment we were born . . . and the eternal one never even blinked an eyelid . . . he watched silently, the sunlight and the storm . . . as the blind struggle in vain, to embrace the will of the Lord . . ."

The words of The Madman echoed in my mind.

~

Walking through the trail of broken promises,

Everything crumbled.

And I stood there,

Watching the ruins of an imagined life,

While the Lord, in all His splendor,

Shone bright in this ever-magical symphony.

Yes, everything would turn into dust,

The dust that reached the farthest corners of the universe,

And the deepest places in your heart.

This is what you will find as you walk,

through the trail of broken promises . . .

the promises that were none but your own.

None but your own.

~

And the mirror cracked.

~

And for the first time, he saw not his own reflection staring back at him but the vast landscape in which was contained everything . . .

It was no mirror.

~

It was the window to eternity.

~

~

Don't pull the trigger. It won't work. Take the gun off your head instead.
There is no hostage.
He appears the moment you put a gun to your head.

~

Throw away your gun.

~

Forever.

~

This is how you really die.

~

I struggled to bring the gun back to my head. It was the only way I knew to live.

~

For a man without a past was also one without a future.

~

My promise of loyalty, His promise of salvation, and my fear of failing Him. This was the trinity of the mind that was now gathering its forces, while the body was writhing in lust for every pleasure it had ever felt.

284

~

This is what happens when you put the gun down, I thought to myself.

~

I usually picked up my weapons with vengeance. But now they were calling out to me.

~

~

I have a question for you.

~

~

Yes. You.

~

~

Who do you think is writing this book?

~

BOOK XXXIV

~

The Invisible Precipice

~

The innocent forget they are waiting.
The innocent leave their dreams behind.
But I never forget. I wait and watch,
never lifting my gaze
even for a moment.
Just like the sea of seas that waits in its wings
for the moment you are ready to be taken.

~

"Time is never wasted. You are never wasted," I heard as I awoke this morning. "Even as all your efforts are in vain."

I laughed, and I cried . . . all at once. And the music was louder than it had ever been.

~

Until every moment is lived with the remembrance of your origin,
time will have its hold on you. And you will live with the curse of hope.

~

I knew today, for the first time in my life, that nothing—not money, or love, or fame, or happiness, or Him—could give me what I was searching for. This was the irrevocable truth from which I was running.

~

Loneliness is divinity imprisoned.

~

"Love . . . It's not in your fabric. You are a self-centered human being."
I was speaking to myself.

"Just who the hell do you think you are, anyway?" I replied. "Do you have even the faintest clue of who or what I really am?"

~

And there was a silence between us.

For the very first time.

~

And it was real. Very real.

~

The Cloud of Thoughts

~

Every word that was ever spoken to me by anyone was me speaking to myself.

And every word that hurt me was already echoing somewhere inside me.

~

There is a time to release all doubt. In God, in Him, but especially, in yourself.

~

Every harsh word that was ever spoken to you was already inside you. Don't raise your weapons at the messenger. For he is none but you. None but you.

~

What pains you is the thorn you carry in your own heart.

~

The first and last step in this game are but one. And distance is the greatest trick ever played by the mind.

~

The gardener tends not only to the youngest sapling, but also to those that are dying.

~

If you believe that one day you will sit on my throne, you are mistaken.

~

It is my throne that shall sit upon you.

~

Real love creates a vast, unimaginable silence . . .
. . . A vast, unimaginable silence creates real love.

~

BOOK XXXV

~

Total acceptance is the greatest power in the universe.

~

Only she deserves to be free who can watch with a smile
as all her bridges burn down. Only she.

~

The journey to the heart of the self is not for the weak or the fearful.

~

There are times you leave yourself so far behind that you pretend to be the
person you were.

~

Just for the sake of continuity.

~

Was I doing this for myself or for the others?
I wondered, even though I knew the answer to that question.

~

The Miracle of Love

~

The darkest moments in your life may reveal to you your greatest truths. For the darker the night gets, the closer you are to your own soul, the silence in your heart, and the demons that you thought you had laid to rest. Stay there . . . stay . . .

~

And one day . . . one day you will shed this skin you wear . . . this skin which carries the history of you. And henceforth will you be the man with no past and no future. You will be . . . the woman, unwritten from the pages of history . . . and from the memories within your heart . . . within your very own heart . . . You will be the woman of the moment.

~

Did you forget that you were the chosen one? Did you forget that you would be . . . the messenger girl? Did you forget . . .

~

So fear not death, my child. Fear not extinction . . . for it is I who waits for you on the other side . . . on the other side . . .

~

And did you forget . . . it is I who can raise the dead from the living . . . and the living from the dead . . . did you forget . . .

~

So cry the unspilled tear, laugh the unheard laugh, and fight the never-fought battle . . . do it all, before you are free . . . do it all, till you are here . . . fighting to stay alive . . .

~

. . . do it all . . . so that nothing remains . . .

~

And the music was so unbearably loud that his eyes closed by themselves.

~

BOOK XXXVI

~

The Offering

~

Wherever you bow down, there He is.
Wherever you touch your palms to the ground, He stands in front of you.
Whoever's feet you touch, He appears.

~

Start with love, the kind that never fades, and whichever direction you move
will take you there.

~

I gift happiness to those who seek freedom.
I gift love to those who seek happiness.
I gift freedom to those who seek love.
And I gift the great emptiness to those who abide in my slavery.

~

Remember, it is I and I alone who knows what you seek.

~

Even when I'm real, I'm faking.
Even I'm faking, I'm real.

~

The Shedding of the Skin

~

I know you want to, but the way to disappear is not to kill yourself. Instead,
find out what you really are. Beyond all that you think and believe.

~

The Never-Ending Circle

~

Every word written in this book comes from your mind, your imagination.

~

How long do want this to go on?

~

Find out where this voice arises from.
Seek its source.

~

But this time I didn't want to find anything out. That was another wild goose chase I was done with. Just like all the others.

"I don't trust you! You play games with me!" I told The Voice in my head.

~

Whatever was to be found would have to be found right here, right now. Or else it would never be.

~

And the chase . . . the hopes and dreams . . . the pain of losing . . . the torture of never being the man you wanted to be would go on, eternally.

~

And those who sought nothing—not love, or riches, or the kingdom of heaven—were already standing there, at the open door.

~

And then he jumped . . .
Or perhaps it was the wind that took him.

298

~

It didn't matter.

He knew that now.

~

You are not the creator.
You are the created.

You see . . . nothing exists but me.

So, in order to create you,
I divided myself into two.

~

He was gone.

~

To become who you truly are, you must fail at who you want to be.

~

BOOK XXXVII

~

The Fragrance of a Flower

~

Wherever the arrow lands, there lies the target.
That's why I make no mistakes.

~

The biggest game your mind can play on you is to work for another's
happiness and freedom when you haven't found your own.

~

Stop converting others.
First convert yourself.

~

Face your deepest desires.
And your greatest fears.

~

The Wounds That Would Never Heal

~

"The problem with realizations is . . ." He said in my dreams. "Like anything in life that's important . . ."

I waited for the answer.

"They can never be taught." He began to walk away. "They must be discovered."

And right then as I woke up . . . right that very second, I discovered something. I understood why He would walk away at the most crucial points in my life.

~

Or make sure I did.

~

"Detachment is a nice word. It's a nice concept. But when it happens, you will run from me," He had said to me, right in the beginning.

But I didn't have to run. I was already far, far away from Him.

~

Arrows may miss their mark. But the fragrance of a flower
always reaches the one whose heart is pure.

~

"It was a test," He said.

"I will keep throwing you out, for some reason or another. It's your job to stay," I remembered Him saying to me sixteen years ago.

I smiled silently.

"You're still standing here. For me," He continued. "Good."

And He turned away to speak to someone else.

~

It felt like many years.

It *was* many years.

~

"If someone gives you everything, isn't it right that you give them everything in return?" My new friend told me at the local bar in Baku the very first time we met.

Who said that? I wondered.

"I can't take credit for that line. It came from somewhere else," He said, with a smile on his face. He knew something was strange about it as well.

"That makes you a messenger, then," I said.

"I wouldn't go that far," He replied.

"But it's the truth." I smiled. "Cheers, anyway." And we drank our spirits till late into the night.

~

Divinity is loneliness embraced.

~

The End of Karma

~

Who was this book for?

It was for the hopeless, who had dreams they believed would never come true.

It was for the outsiders, who wanted to get away from this world more than anything else.

It was for the heartbroken, unable to recover from a love that had consumed them.

It was for the alcoholics, who found their solace in wine and wine alone.

It was for the addicted, who needed a way to escape this world.

It was for the self-destructive, who were moving faster toward death than the others.

It was for the crazy ones, who couldn't distinguish the real from the false.

It was for the strange ones, who lived in a world far away from the one they encountered every day.

It was for the guilty—the ones who carried a burden they believed they deserved to carry.

It was for the losers—the ones who had failed themselves or someone dear to them.

~

But it was also for the fighters, struggling with faith, as they never stopped fighting for what they believed in.

It was for the lovers, who cared not for time and space and convenience.

It was for seekers of the truth, who had embarked on a dangerous journey.

It was for the courageous, who never put their weapons down.

It was for the single-minded, who could not be swayed by temptation . . . that came in many, many forms.

It was for the ones who could laugh at anything.

It was for the ones who could smile even as their homes came crumbling down.

It was for the ones who embraced their death, for they knew it was coming sooner rather than later.

~

It was for me.

~

And depression was nothing but a war with loneliness.

~

Who was I? The question remained.

Some days I was The Leper, still wondering where The Captain was taking us and still waiting to be called upon.

Some days I was The Madman, whom no one, including myself, could understand.

Some days I was The Lute Player, eternally waiting for love.

Some days I was The Lead Shipman, who found his peace in obeying The Captain's commands.

Some days I was The Captain himself.

Some days, I . . .

~

Yes, I.

~

Was the King of the Sea.

~

BOOK XXXVIII

~

He had kept them hidden in his bunker, behind the wooden slates on the sides. But one day he told me about them late at night when we were talking about the book I had once found.

"I, too, have something that no one has seen on this ship," he said, taking out his drawings, made with charcoal.

"They're beautiful," I said, looking at the strange shapes and figures.

"They are from my dreams," The Lead Shipman said. "Or from a place I must have seen before."

But The Lead Shipman was the strongest on the ship. He had a job to do. So what he drew was hardly important. That's why he never showed them to anyone. Until today, when the ship was in the air.

~

A Thousand Ways to Read a Book

~

We met at the old farm by the hillock. She came to tell me that this was all a waste of time and that I should do whatever it takes to find my happiness. I heard the words as if from a distance. They were the truest words I could have heard, and yet they skimmed my mind and heart and vanished into the thin air like the clouds above.

And even though she said what she had come to say, we sat near the tree, holding hands, feeling the moment in all its purity and splendor. For we both knew in our heart of hearts that, even though everything would change, nothing had really changed. But even moments as pure as this could scar you forever. For you knew they would never, ever repeat . . .

After all, a real goodbye could be as powerful and as beautiful as the first time you met someone you loved.

~

One Hundred and Thirty-Six Seconds

~

That's how long The Lute Player fell through the skies before he hit the ground.

~

That's how long my father had after he decided to land his failed Mig-21 on the 25th of November, 1972, away from a school full of children, till the plane burst into flames, killing him instantly.

~

That was how long he had danced with her at her wedding.

~

The Beginning and the End

~

He was a young man, maybe thirty-five years old. He looked a lot younger, and he was tall, with a boyish but handsome face.

"Can I tell you something?" he asked, as we drove through the streets of Paris, on the way to the airport.

"Sure." I was in a quiet mood today.

"I sometimes see things before they happen."

I listened quietly.

"My family gets scared sometimes," he continued. "What's the explanation . . . do you know?"

Why was he asking me this, I wondered . . . I had met him only a few minutes ago.

"You don't know it, but you've meditated a lot," I replied. "Things are coming to you."

He listened carefully.

"Ignore all these things, and be focused on your destination."

"What's that?" he said to me, without saying a word.

"Where we come from," I said. "Where we have to get back."

~

Be careful when you want to free yourself from time.
Many things rush toward you. Many things.
Be especially careful of the door that promises you heaven.

~

Could this book be one of those doors? I wondered.

~

Sometimes it's the one thing that keeps you from disappearing.

~

There was something I was about to write. But as I started typing in the words, I realized I had already written them. It sounded like something I wrote in the first chapter.

I scrolled quickly.

There it was.

I had already written it . . . a few years ago.

~

It was exactly what I was going to write.

~

"So, what are you going to do now with your life? And where will you go?"
I was speaking to myself.

"I don't know."

"You have to do something. Anything."

"I don't know. I really don't."

I was quiet.

"Not knowing is the answer. Living in the mystery can have mysterious effects on your life," The Voice spoke.

I was quiet.

"The universe can't react to you anymore. It needs you to know or want something in order to react to it."

"What happens then?"

"See for yourself. Don't you enjoy being surprised?"

I smiled. "I do."

~

BOOK XXXIX

~

I Will Rise

~

For a foolish man to be hated is one thing.
For a wise man, it is another matter entirely.

~

Where was he?

~

"I didn't speak to you for more than a year,' The Voice said.

"Yes," I said. I hadn't written a word for more than a year.

"You thought you wouldn't ever publish this book, didn't you?"

"Yes. I had completely forgotten about it," I replied.

"Good that you dropped it."

"Yes."

~

Don't forget—ever—that it is I who does everything.

~

And don't forget another thing.
I don't need you.
I chose you.

~

And so the story continued. And the flying ship sailed till eternity.

~

"So take your places, and row with all your might, as you are used to doing. For this ship is the only way into the kingdom of the eternal," The King said, sitting on top of the deck with a glass of wine in his hands. "We must race against time, and beat it, for time and time alone is our greatest enemy."

They listened silently.

And as they took their places on the ship, far away somewhere, I heard the song in my head . . .

"Hold on to your sails,

You will not lose me.

Hold on to your sails,

It's time to be free.

Looking for nothing, he stands,

The King of the Sea.

You are the chosen one,

Eternally."

~

You seek resolution. I gift silence.

~

Enter the Godhead

~

And so began the reign of the King, whose kingdom grew with every defeat and whose borders broke into the hardest of hearts.

~

"You, too, will be the Captain of your ship one day," The Captain had said to him a long time ago.

His ship was waiting for him at the port. Patiently.

For little did he know that even ships had souls and they sometimes waited for a thousand years before their Captain was ready to climb in and take his seat.

~

A real Captain always enters his ship alone. Always.

~

He learns how to sail his ship without a single shipman.

~

He knew how to tie the sails all by himself. He knew how to read the charts and the stars. He knew how to fish and cook his fish. He knew how to stay alone in his cabin for years—or decades, if he had to.

~

But he also knew how to make the shipmen dance . . . and sing . . . and play . . . and work.

~

Truly, The Captain loved his shipmen more than anything else in the world.

~

A Lifetime Too Late

~

"Love and hate, Nandan," He had said, waving His hands as He usually did when he spoke. "Both are good."

I had listened carefully.

"It's indifference you must watch out for."

~

> *First I create love.*
> *Then I gift the wound.*
> *Then I heal the wound.*

~

That's when you are empty.

~

And as I drifted away from the house and the village, I felt it stronger than ever . . . Even if it was a lifetime too late.

Whether I had truly loved her or not hardly mattered now.

That I had forgotten I loved my brother, did.

~

The greatest paradox was that people who believed they had loved the most were actually the most incapable of love.

For they hadn't begun to love themselves.

They had never truly embraced their loneliness.

Till today.

Till today.

~

How did I know this?

~

Because I was one of them. And I was now wise enough to know that whatever words I spoke, were always . . .

. . . always for myself.

Some yearn for immortality.
Some race toward their death.
Others simply disappear.
They escape themselves.

~

The Day the Tears Began to Flow

~

I sat next to him on the staircase of the old building where my mother lived.

It was the summer of Nineteen Ninety-Nine.

My head was spinning. Nothing felt real anymore. The whole of life was some kind of a game. It was God's little playground, and we were the actors.

I could see it that day, so clear and so obvious, and there was as much pain as there was peace.

And suddenly, after more than a decade, I burst into tears. I had forgotten what it was like to cry. Everything around me was crumbling, and there was nothing I could do about it. Absolutely nothing.

He put his hand on my back.

"Don't worry," He said. "It will all be fine. It will all be fine."

In my twenty-eight years, I hadn't heard a voice as reassuring as His was today. Not only because He loved me. But because I knew He knew the truth. He had to. For it was only because of Him that I had gotten a glimpse of it . . . a glimpse that I could never forget. One that would haunt me forever.

He became my Master from that very day. In that moment.

And I knew I could trust Him with my life.

~

And nothing—nothing—would ever change that.

~

My love for you is eternal and will always be.

~

Initiation

~

And that night as I lay down on my bed and closed my eyes, I saw a thousand lights shining bright, like little suns and diamonds, dancing a cosmic dance, right in front of my eyes. A sense of peace rushed through me, as if I had seen, for a moment, the force behind all that we see around us.

~

To the void and beyond, shall we go, my friend.
To the void and within, shall we fall, my friend.
To the void and away, shall we fly, my friend
To the void and never the same, shall we be, my friend.
Cheers to the void, and beyond.
For this is the place where you and I disappear, and only
I will remain, my friend.
Only I will remain.

~

Yes, I will rise.

~

I must.

~

As all of you, today or tomorrow, will be dead and gone,
And I will remain.

~

Therefore,
Today or tomorrow . . .

~

I Will Rise.

~

The Divine Flaw

~

He knew that very moment what had actually happened. The very moment he kissed Yeshua's cheek. It wasn't the kiss of betrayal. It was an indication that the disciple had followed the Master's orders.

Yes, he was told by Yeshua to do what he did. He never wished to betray Him—for a few silver coins, at that. There was no glory or honor in that. He already knew this. He was a man of superior intelligence. But to obey the Master was a vow he had taken to himself many years ago.

And as much as he loved Yeshua, he also despised one thing about Him. Why was He the chosen one?

Why was it not himself? Was he not good enough for the Lord?

And so he realized in that moment that Yeshua allowed him his vengeance. He allowed him his anger.

But now that he knew this, there was no way to forget it. And so the burden would have to be carried. By him. And so he believed that his time on this planet, like Yeshua's, was over.

And he took the rope, placed it around his neck, and prayed to Yeshua for forgiveness. Not for betraying him, but for hating him. For hating the son of God, for any reason, was unacceptable, in his own eyes.

He knew all of this in that single kiss. His imperfect love for Yeshua. And Yeshua's perfect love for him. And he knew then, in that very moment, why the Lord had chosen Yeshua and not him.

And with that thought, he was gone.

And destined to be the most hated man to walk the planet. For betrayal was a crime higher than any other. And the betrayal of your Master was the highest of all betrayals.

And as his soul left the body, he fulfilled his contract with Yeshua. And in those last few moments, he believed he had made his peace with the Lord, and with Yeshua—the son of God, and the son of man.

~

My story never ends.
Yours always does.

~

I was helped practically every step of the way. Throughout my life. Especially when I needed it the most.

I had achieved nothing.

Nothing at all.

~

See through yourself.
I see through you.

~

"How did you do this?" someone asked me. "Did you ever learn music?"
"Tried and failed. Several times," I said. "So I kept listening . . . for thirty years."
"Then?"
"One fine day, it began to flow . . . outwards."

~

Only when you know what love is not,
Can you know what love is . . .

Only when you leave behind your idea of beauty,
Will you be able to see it everywhere . . .

Only when you have not a single reason to serve yourself,
Can you serve others . . .

~

The Broken Contracts

~

No contract is ever broken. It only awaits its fulfillment. One way or another.

~

And with that, there was nothing more that could be revealed.
And nothing that wasn't already.

~

August 31, 2016

~

And The Captain continued to sit every night in his cabin, peering into the charts, looking at his compass, making his calculations . . . making sure the ship never came anywhere close to land. Not in a thousand years.

~

Never.

~

It was the only way.

~

BOOK XL

~

The Man With No Life

~

"Why can't you just be happy?" she said, in my dreams.

I was quiet. Somewhere along the way, perhaps a long time ago, I had begun to look down upon happiness. After all, it was a fleeting emotion, without any real foundation—a moment of comfort or pleasure that could be pulled from under your feet at any time. And this feeling had seeped into my bones now. It was an intrinsic part of me. It was me.

It's not my thing, I thought to myself. But I wasn't fully satisfied with that answer. For I knew that it had taken away from my life as much as it had given.

~

Time appears because you seek an experience.

~

I counted the days. It had been more than seventeen years since I boarded the ship.

Finally, there was nowhere to go, and nothing to leave. I sat on the upper deck quietly staring into the sunset and the clouds when I felt someone walk behind me.

~

You think you're going to lose me?

~

What a joke . . .

~

I was listening.

~

I will be the one to lose you.

~

What a load of nonsense . . . I thought to myself as I looked back on all that I had written.

~

Perhaps I was being a bit harsh. But still.

What was my objective here?

Was it to express myself? To make money? Or be famous?

The fact was—I had no real reason at all. And the ones I did have weren't good enough.

~

I had two choices now: Either delete everything I had written and be rid of it forever. Or else keep it exactly as it was for whatever it was worth.

~

Stories are nice. They can teach you things. Imagination has its place. But they prevent you from seeing life as it truly is, in its innocence and purity. The truth is that we prefer to be transported somewhere else. Somewhere unreal, where we can lead a parallel life that has no connection to the reality of the present moment.

~

We create in order to destroy.

~

It was true . . . I had gone far away from myself.

~

Far away.

~

But some things were like that.
I had no choice in this matter.

~

This book would be published. And life would lead me to my true destination
no matter what I did or didn't do.

~

This is what I believed. And nothing could change that.

~

Once upon a time . . .

~

*Once upon a time, perhaps in my dreams, she had whispered to me in my ear,
"Don't let me go."*
And so I couldn't.

~

And so I didn't.

~

Until today, when my hands that held the only sails I knew, found themselves loosening their grip on the wood, leaving behind all that was dear to me, good and bad, painful and happy.

~

And this time, no song played in my heart. And the silence swelled like it would swallow me whole.

~

November 24, 2016

~

Hide in plain sight, my friend.
I hide in plain sight.

~

Once you've seen through love, don't look back.
Don't hanker for the joys of an old habit.

~

Every circle completes itself. As your life eventually will.
Embrace where you have come to, no matter where you are.

~

Remember, all beginnings begin with loss.
As all healing must begin with a wound.

~

"I don't need your loyalty," He said, in my dreams. "Just do the right thing.
And you will have my respect."

~

I woke up.
What was right? And whose respect was I really trying to earn?

~

Who Am I

~

"Who are you?" The Voice asked me that night as I slept.
"Who am I?" I asked myself.
But instead of an answer, the words echoed through my mind, bouncing off
every wall in this empty room, again and again, until they disappeared. And
what remained was the one who had asked the question. And the one who
could not answer.

~

They were one and the same.

~

And I.

Yes, I. Was the King of the Sea.

The sea of thoughts and desires,

The sea of longings and punishments.

The sea of hopes and guilt,

The sea of love and disloyalties.

The sea of betrayal and forgiveness,

The sea of laughter and tears.

The sea of successes and failures,

The sea of magic and logic.

I was the ship that carried them. And just as they were free to live inside me if they so wished, I, too, was free to live with or without them. After all, it was they who needed me to exist. I didn't need them.

I was already here.

~

Long before they arrived.

~

January 9, 2017

BOOK XLI

~

Anatomy of Enlightenment

~

Either say yes to everything,
or say no to everything.
The true self is revealed.

~

He would disturb the very essence of her peace,
Knowing that she would receive something far more valuable than all that
she had strived to become.
It was nothing anyway, she knew.
For in the presence of the One, everything dissolved.

~

Who was this I was seeing?

Was it someone I knew . . . or someone I would meet in the future . . .

~

It was all there in the contract.

The contract that each of us had chosen.

Chosen, without a doubt.

~

For the contract was nothing but a path to our eternal freedom.

No matter how painful it had been.

No matter how painful it could be.

No matter how painful it had appeared to be.

~

It was the only way.

~

Till you are separate, love can be experienced.
Once you are one, everything disappears.

For truly, though one can hate oneself,
Or appear to,

One cannot love oneself.
For that, you would have to be two.

~

If you want to live in the presence of greatness,
Learn how to live with your head bowed down.

~

"Your book's personal," said a friend. "Maybe too personal."

"It will soon be out for the world to see." I said, with a smile. "Nothing is really personal anyway. I can hardly identify with myself as the writer . . ."

I looked out of the window, watching people strolling down my street, and the cars driving by in a rush. *It's all fiction. All of it,* I thought to myself, feeling like a character . . . in a dream that was sure to end one day.

~

Watch out.
The ones who enter the room quietly
also leave quietly.

~

You start with the watching.
You end as the watcher.

~

Only the One
Ever existed.

Only the One
Exists.

Only the One
Will ever exist.

~

I point the way forward.
And I also lead you away.
For truth is neither given nor taken.

~

And there he was, walking once again by the lakes and the trees, looking at the blue skies and the birds as if for the first time. It was a new day. It was a new land.

He hadn't died.

He couldn't.

~

Each time he let go of the ship.

Or was thrown off.

Or was taken by the wave.

Or by the winds.

~

Or each time he left home.

Each time he left Him.

And each time she left him.

It made absolutely no difference.

~

He could not disappear.

No matter how much he wanted to.

~

No matter how many times he had tried in the past or would in the future.

~

He knew today, without a doubt . . .

~

That he could never die.

~

He was immortal.

~

March 2, 2017

EPILOGUE

~

He saw it happen. The others were all busy, down below, in the lower deck. And he saw it, with his very own eyes. He saw The Captain push The Lute Player off the side of the ship for no good reason.

How could he do that? he thought to himself. How could he do that to the one man who had stayed by his side for so long . . . The only reason he himself hadn't jumped off this ship was because, many years ago, he had heard The Captain say to The Lute Player, "Never let go of the ship. Never." And he believed it was as much for him as it was for The Lute Player.

He would never forget that day. Never.

But today, it was he himself, The Captain, who threw his best friend off this ship.

Now there was truly nothing to live for. Not one reason to be alive, even if this flying ship was about to reach land.

Because nothing mattered anymore. Nothing.

And so, when The Captain walked away after a quick glance in his direction, as if he knew all too well that he was watching, The Leper took one last look at the ship and another look at his rotting hands, before he slowly hobbled to the closest edge and, without a moment's hesitation, jumped off the ship.

~

"I will see you soon, my friend," was the last thought that passed through his mind as he fell through the skies . . .

~

That night, when The Winemaker noticed that neither The Lute Player nor The Leper was present while the men drank and danced, he asked gently, to anyone who may have heard his voice, "Has anyone seen The Leper or The Lute Player?"

"Don't bother looking for them . . . they are gone," The Captain replied, from the other end of the lower deck.

"But how could this be?" he asked, unable to accept The Captain's words.

"It is so," The Captain replied again. "It just is."

"But I have no one left to cheer and make happy," he said, his face falling like never before. "They were my only real friends."

"You have yourself," The Captain said out loud. "Cheer yourself up. For that is what you were born to do, was it not?"

The Winemaker stood silent, trying his best to take in what he had just heard.

~

Whatever makes you come alive is the path.

~

I woke up this morning, feeling as terrible as I could ever have. For no reason at all. I didn't want anything more from life . . . not one thing. And yet, I was unhappy today. Everything felt meaningless and empty.

Why was peace so elusive?

Why did I keep slipping back?

Was this pain even mine? I began to wonder.

~

I wanted something. It wasn't anything specific. But it was right around the corner.

I knew it. I felt it.

And yet, it always remained . . . right around the corner.

~

You're looking for a moment in time.
Perhaps a bolt of lightning.
Or something like that.

~

I was.

~

Yes. I was.

I hated to admit it. But as ridiculous as it sounded, it was true.

~

That's never going to happen.
And you know exactly why.

~

I did.

~

She found herself washing her hair that day. It wasn't a Sunday morning as it should have been. But today, she simply had to do it. It meant nothing actually, she told herself. But when you've done something for years, perhaps decades . . . and then one day for no rhyme or reason, you break the habit, it makes you stop in your tracks. Freedom would be an arduous journey, she knew. A long, arduous one.

But there was freedom in living an ordinary life. Yes . . . an ordinary life is what she would lead. A life so ordinary, that she would have to be free exactly where she was, without running away to a single place.

Ever.

~

It was the same girl I had seen earlier.

~

The only way to gift you the music,
Was for you to create it.

~

How questions changed with time . . . For years, all The Lute player could think about was whether she had truly loved him. He needed her love then.

And for years he had wondered if he had loved her at all. He needed to know whether he was capable of it . . .

338

~

But he knew now that these questions had no answers.

He could believe whatever he wanted to, of course. But that would change nothing.

After all, believing and being were two different things. You cannot believe in love, he thought to himself as he drifted through some strange land that would perhaps, in time, become his home.

~

That would be like believing in God.

~

It was not a moment in time. It was a choice to make at every moment . . . every single moment.

~

Relationships fail not because of separation.
And succeed not from being together.
They are measured by the love that you are able to bear in your heart.

~

And The Lute Player's music, with all its imperfections, still carried the sacred blessings, the deafening silence . . . and the joy and pain that could heal a thousand hearts.

It cut through the landscape, through time . . . like a river through the hills and the valleys . . . to finally reach the bottom of the ocean, from whence it came.

~

March 20, 2017

ABOUT THE AUTHOR

~

Nandan Gautam grew up in Bangalore, India.
He completed his Liberal Arts degree from McDaniel College,
Maryland, USA and worked at newspaper USA Today for a few
years. He returned to India to study yoga and meditation for the
next twenty years under spiritual master Bharat Thakur.

His journey of self-discovery led him back to his first love –
music, where he infuses his raw but ethereal vocals with
hypnotic rhythms and harmonies specifically designed to
calm, heal and transform the self.

A Lie and a Truth, an anthology of conversations and life
experiences with his master, was his first book. *The King of the Sea*
is his first novel and music album. He lives in Baku, Azerbaijan.

Flying

(For my Mother)

~

Don't know where I'm going but it's fast
The answer to a question I had asked

This is where the river meets the sea
Don't know what is happening to me

Is this just a story I have lived
Is there anything that I can give

I close my eyes, there's nothing there to see
Visions disappearing to eternity...

~

There's nothing here for me but here I am
It looks like everything was always planned

So never run away from who you are
Stop lying to yourself, you've come too far

You've washed away the darkness in the rain
You've lived your share of misery and pain

Stop worrying now and know that you are free
Just look around there's no one else but me...

~

Once upon a time there was a man
Everything that happened looks like lines in the sand...

~

There's something you don't know about this place
It's lonely so I wore a different face

So how about just living for me now
We're just one growing family one race

You think one day you know what you'll become
It's up to you but try to have some fun

It's hard to see that death is but a friend
I've seen the future, you're coming with me to the end...

~

~

"Smile, all creatures from all races,
It is my tears that stream down your faces,
Come with me. Come away,
For I shall take you to the place beyond all places."

~